Samuél Lopez-Barrantes

CW01091592

The
REQUISITIONS

kingdom
anywhere

Praise for *The Requisitions*

"Vibrant, shadowed, compelling and ultimately symphonic, *The Requisitions* offers the gift of love in an impossible situation. What starts in a Polish town in a cafe in 1939 ends in the hearts of readers, everywhere, now. Moving and, as intended, memorable."

—Nor Hall, author of *The Moon and The Virgin* and *Those Women*

"The sorrowing starkness of Albrecht Durer haunts this account of a Europe overshadowed by the imminent avalanche of history, a cataclysm its characters feel helpless, even unwilling to avert."

—John Baxter, author of *The Most Beautiful Walk in the World*

"There is an inherent lyricism throughout this original and ambitious novel. Deeply researched and masterfully constructed, *The Requisitions* traces the lives of captivating characters and leaves us with a deep sense of having traversed an arduous and unforgettable journey—during World War Two and beyond."

—Heather Hartley, author of *Knock Knock* and *Adult Swim*

"Riveting reading. *The Requisitions* never lets the reader feel the safe distance of history. The result is viscerally uncomfortable—and perhaps this is necessary for the memory of the Holocaust to remain present and real within us."

—Tim Ward, author of *Mature Flâneur*

"*The Requisitions* is houndlike and astute. Its ambition is a dance with our expectations, a toast to the venerable traditions of the book."

—Stokes Prickett, the mysterious author of *Foodie*

"Masterful prose and plotting, and a unique and imaginative approach, blending personal memoir, historical metafiction, and philosophical inquiry into the deepest recesses of the human soul...sobering, unsettling...but comes out—barely—on the side of a case for hope."

—Janet Hulstrand, author of *Demystifying The French*

"A roadmap through some of the most dangerous and emotional moments of our time. This page-turning book is a must-read for all those who value the work of a master storyteller in command of his material."

—David A. Andelman, author of *A Shattered Peace: Versailles 1919 and the Price We Pay Today*

SAMUÉL LOPEZ-BARRANTES lives in Paris. He hosts a literary salon, teaches creative writing at the Sorbonne, and leads historical walks on modernism, existentialism, and the Nazi Occupation of Paris.

The Requisitions is Samuél Lopez-Barrantes' second novel. His first novel, *Slim and The Beast* (Inkshares, 2015), is a coming-of-age story about a college basketball player and a war veteran set in Chapel Hill, North Carolina.

samuellopezbarrantes.com

Kingdom Anywhere Publishing
Paris, France

First published in France by Kingdom Anywhere Publishing, 2024
Copyright © Samuél Lopez-Barrantes 2024

ISBN 979-8-9895803-0-9 (paperback)
ISBN 979-8-9895803-1-6 (eBook)

Cover Illustration: Saskia Meiling
Editorial: Carrie Chappell, Augusta Sagnelli

First American Edition

For permissions or information: kingdomanywherepub@gmail.com

Contents

requisition

[noun]

1. The act of formally requiring or calling upon someone to perform an action

2. A demand or application made, usually with authority

3. The state of being in demand or use

From Latin, *requisitio*, the act of searching; from *requirere*, to seek, to ask

Merriam-Webster Online Dictionary

a boy at a bookshelf

I sit in one of the dives
On Fifty-second Street
Uncertain and afraid
As the clever hopes expire
Of a low dishonest decade:
Waves of anger and fear
Circulate over the bright
And darkened lands of the earth,
Obsessing our private lives;
The unmentionable odor of death
Offends the September night.

—WH Auden, "September 1 1939"

When the sirens begin, the professor is sitting at the Astoria Café. Professor Viktor Bauman's clean-shaven face accentuates his smile. Though he's only a figment of my imagination, he reminds me of myself as a child, sliding the crystal pepper shaker back and forth between his hands atop the white linen tablecloth (today, like yesterday, the waiter has forgotten the salt).

This is when Viktor first sees her, the young woman in the burgundy dress, smiling at him from across the terrace. Her name is Elsa Dietrich—she is of my imagination, too—and she is about to receive some troubling news concerning her estranged fiancé, Carl. I can hear the clinking of teaspoons on serving plates and the conversations at the bar. Elsa listens to a bald man with a gruff voice criticize Professor Bauman's optimism about the situation. It is September 1, 1939, and black smoke is billowing on the horizon, but for some reason, Professor Viktor Bauman is not afraid.

The Astoria Café really did exist. It was a haven for artists and thinkers during the 1930s in the otherwise industrial town of Łódź, Poland. My mother often told me the story of how my obsession with this history began: I was just a boy, no taller than a fire hydrant, when I first looked up at the bookshelf, tall and white, which lorded over the wooden cabinets filled with trinkets and old toys. As the story goes, I climbed onto the cabinets, stood on my tiptoes, and pulled down a thick black book with red ink scrawled on the spine, William L. Shirer's *The Rise and Fall of the Third Reich*.

From that moment onwards, I became obsessed. I collected books, action figures, DVDs, military medals, anything that might help me understand the calamity of World War Two. I watched (and re-watched) *Nuit et Brouillard*, *Life is Beautiful*, *Schindler's List*, and *Saving Private Ryan*. I played every video game I could find, mastering *Medal of Honor* and *Company of Heroes* and *Brothers in Arms*, hoping that sooner or later I'd understand what it was like to live through those times. The obsession stayed with me through university and graduate school—a degree in Holocaust studies, another in the psychology of genocide—but the more I studied, the less I understood. What did that little boy at the bookshelf know that I could no longer remember?

Another memory of me peering at that bookshelf, this time as a graduate student home for Christmas: I'd woken up early, before the real-estate appraisers came, to help my mother sort through the cabinets beneath the bookshelf (she was bankrupt and had to sell the house; the measly family fortune had all been spent treating her mother's Alzheimer's). The trouble was, my mom tended towards hoarding. If it were up to her, she'd hold onto everything, so I agreed, begrudgingly, to spend the days between Christmas and New Year's sorting through it all.

That morning, I sat on the living room floor surrounded by boxes. I sifted through old memories of stiff plastic action figures, faded Lincoln Logs, chewed-up Legos and dog-eared textbooks, trying to be as categorical as possible while my mother cleared out pots and pans in the kitchen. Her long-term memory was faltering, but still, few people were more attuned to their primordial wisdom than she.

"You sure you don't want to keep that?" She pointed at a clay sculpture of a dog.

"It's broken."

"You made it at art camp in the Great Smoky Mountains."

"Wasn't it in Maine?"

"No," she picked up the three-legged dog. "I'd like to hold onto this if you don't mind. It's the first piece of art you ever made. One day, your grandchildren will thank me."

"We've already talked about this. I don't want children."

The words cast a shadow on her face. "I'd like to keep it anyway. Someday, you might want to remember."

"What do you mean, remember?"

"This sculpture is a totem, son. It's evidence of who you were—of who you are. You're too categorical about the past—you think it's finished. No, don't put it there.

Thank you, I'll keep it. You can be so dismissive. There's still something you need to remember, son."

My mother looked at the growing discard pile and picked up an old set of dominoes in a red leather case. She shook her head and pulled out three ivory pieces that rattled in her hand as she contemplated their weight.

"These used to belong to your grandfather, you know. He fought for the Republicans during the Spanish Civil War. Do you know the story of the night Franco's police came knocking at his door? The euphemism was simple enough: *dar un paseo*. Most who were 'given a walk' never came home."

"But Granddad survived the war."

"Yes. Because of these dominoes," she held out her hand. "When your grandfather was arrested, he was allowed one personal item. For some reason, he brought the dominoes to the station. One of his captors recognized it—he'd had one just like it in grade school. They got to talking. Eventually, he let your grandfather go."

My mother returned the ivory pieces to the red leather case and snapped it shut. "Son, be careful what you decide to forget. Getting it back isn't as easy as you might think."

Barely aware of what she was trying to tell me, we continued sorting through the artifacts of my childhood, moving from the cabinets up to the bookshelf, where she pulled down the tattered copy of *The Rise and Fall of the Third Reich* and put it in a trash bag.

"We can't give *that* one away," I said.

"Don't you have a copy?"

"Yes, but this one's different," I pulled it out.

"Oh, *is* it?" She grinned. "I remember you standing on

the cabinets on your tiptoes, holding that very book in your hands, just like you're doing now. I'd never seen anything like it, a little boy wanting to read about *that*."

I turned the book over in my hand. "Why'd I choose this one?"

"You don't remember?"

"No."

"You said they needed your help."

"Who?"

And that's when they came back to me, Viktor and Elsa.

Viktor's eyes are obscured by a black suede hat that complements the colorful scarf he's looped around his neck for warmth and display. Here on the terrace, he feels a world away from the industrial sprawl of unpaved roads, textile plants, and rundown tenements to the north of the city. Though Viktor doesn't wear glasses, he still looks the part of an academic, which means that today, like yesterday, he's procrastinating. Already on his second cup of coffee, he's come to the Astoria not to write but to people-watch until his friend Martin arrives.

Crisp days like today remind Viktor of autumn afternoons at Kings College; cups of tea on Euston Square; passionate conversations at the pub over pints of lager and shots of whiskey; of walking with Helen through Paris' Latin Quarter, the last time he felt at home. Though Łódź isn't Paris, Viktor comes to the Astoria to appreciate its baroque décor and the warm hues of gold and red, which recall the packed terraces of Montparnasse.

But the past has passed. Viktor is in his mid-thirties

now. *Focus on the good things, Viktor.* Yes, today feels like a good day again: the skies are still blue, and the woman in the burgundy dress is back, and is she smiling at him again? As soon as he catches her eye, Viktor looks away. He knows her from somewhere, but how? She's far too elegant to be a university student. Viktor is mesmerized by how intensely she scribbles words into her notebook. *If only I had the discipline.*

Viktor tries to refocus on his papers, on what he's scribbled under the title, "A Treatise on Aesthetics," but his mind won't fix. He can never get any work done at the café anyway, and he's far more interested in what the woman in the burgundy dress is writing in *her* notebook.

Viktor steals a glance as she brushes her hair behind her ear. *Did she look at me? This time, I'm sure of it.* Viktor looks away again, grabs the crystal pepper shaker, and slides it from hand to hand atop the white linen, sprinkling black specks across the clean surface.

Viktor's closest friend in the city, Martin Arendt, soon arrives with his wispy gray hair and round belly.

"Pretending to write again, are we, *professor?*" Martin slaps Viktor on the back and takes a seat. The wrinkles around Martin's eyes suggest a long history of smiling, but today, his face is marked by a tired scowl.

Martin rubs his belly, lights a cigarette, and glares at the woman in the burgundy dress. "And who, let me guess, are you trying to impress? That's five days now that she's been watching us. You still don't have a name?"

"You're paranoid, Martin. She isn't *watching* anyone. Anyway, I'd rather try to impress *her* than a group of stuffy

academics. Can you believe I've been working on this treatise for five years, and I can't even think of a decent first
sentence?"

"No, frankly, I can't. You're an idiot. Why do you still
care about aesthetics? The answer is easy: it's all subjective,
and the rest has already been said."

"Sure," Viktor smiles. "Except nobody ever listens."

"You've got that right," Martin scoots his chair forward
until his belly is pressed against the table's edge. "Did you
learn that after the first or *second* master's degree?"

Viktor laughs and looks over at the mysterious woman.
She averts her eyes and focuses on spooning her cold beet
soup, bravely cupping her white-gloved hand beneath the
crimson Chłodnik as she brings it to her lips.

"She's been eavesdropping, you know," Martin doesn't
bother whispering.

"What's wrong with you," Viktor hisses. "You're going
to scare her away."

"You can't trust anyone these days," Martin says.
"Speaking of, where's Calel? He forgot to put out the salt
again, didn't he? That boy's a liability, I tell you."

"Don't be so hard on him. He's anxious enough as it is."

"Better he learn it from us than *them*." Martin takes a
long drag of his cigarette and puffs a cloud of smoke in the
young woman's direction. "I've got a joke for you, Viktor.
Ready? A man walks into a bar."

"Okay."

"His alcohol dependency is destroying his family."

Martin laughs from his belly, shaking the table's edge.
Viktor smiles and turns towards the café's interior to flag

down the rosy-cheeked, gangly, bow-tied waiter.

Calel stumbles to the table with a tray of coffee, which he promptly spills all over the pristine white linen. Martin has no time to move before the black liquid has seeped to the table's edge, staining his belly.

Martin takes another long drag of his cigarette. "Good morning, Calel. First spill of the day? You almost made it to lunch this time."

"I'm incredibly sorry, Mr. Arendt. It won't happen again. Here, let me help."

"It has and it will. A dry napkin is useless! Bring me something damp, you buffoon."

The sheepish waiter disappears into the restaurant and returns, trembling, with a damp rag.

Viktor places his hand on Calel's shoulder and passes the cloth to Martin. "Calel, why don't you take a seat? It's fine. Just calm down."

Words tumble from Calel's mouth before his frail body hits the chair. "My daughter is sick, and what with the *Luftwaffe* strafing refugees outside of Warsaw, I don't know *what* to believe anymore … you've heard the rumors, haven't you, professor? About what they're doing to Polish babies? They'll be here tomorrow, the next day at best. I can't let my daughter and wife … I do … do you think I should …"

"Calm, Calel," Viktor squeezes his shoulder. "If we haven't been bombed yet, it's for good reason, right?"

"Ah, now *that's* wisdom from the great *Professor Bauman*," Martin bellows. "If we haven't been bombed yet, it *is* for good reason: Poland is already *kaput*."

"Nonsense," Viktor dismisses the thought. "You're

just being a grumpy old man. The Łódź Army is holding strong."

Martin tosses the soiled rag onto Viktor's empty cup of coffee. "Your youthful optimism will get us killed. Mark my words. Nazis on our doorstep and you're speaking like a theorist. What does an optimist have to say about the SS and the Death's Head?"

"Have some faith, Martin. We're still drinking coffee, aren't we? And tomorrow we'll drink again. For now, that stain on your shirt needs some salt."

"The salt," Calel slumps his shoulders. "I forgot to put it out. Tomasz is going to kill me."

"Sit. I'll get it." Viktor enters the café for two saltshakers, one for his table, the other for the woman in the red dress.

A bicyclist in a gas mask passes the terrace and rings his bell at a young couple shoving suitcases into the trunk of a small car. The cyclist pulls off his mask to force a smile and wish the couple luck. Elsa has been watching similar scenes for days: locals contorting their faces to make believe they'll be safe in the city while others flee in terror towards another kind of unknown. But Elsa is German, and her estranged fiancé is in the army, and rumors suggest the city won't be bombarded. Despite the sirens, Elsa has decided to adopt the professor's optimism and remain seated at her usual table to write about the goings-on at the café: *The waiter's passivity reminds me of Carl. He managed to contact me at the hotel. He's still hundreds of miles away, but I keep seeing him in the face of unfriendly strangers. At least he's stopped sending me letters … the invasion will keep him occupied. The professor smiled at me again today. I want to say hello. He seems comfortable in his boyishness. A man of levity. Quite accomplished for a professor not yet in his forties. His older friend, Martin, is a retired chess master; he was particularly cranky when Viktor beat him. The same couple from yesterday is now arriving at the professor's table. Rachel is a painter—I like her spirit—and Tadeusz is a carpenter. He's a bit too brooding and moody.*

"Excuse me, mademoiselle?"

Elsa looks up from the page to see the professor standing before her with a saltshaker.

"He always forgets the salt," Viktor grins.

"Thank you, professor," she says with an almost native Polish accent. "I don't believe we've met."

"Bauman. Professor Viktor Bauman."

Viktor takes off his hat and gives Elsa an exaggerated bow. "Or at least that's what they used to call me. Classes have been postponed indefinitely, so for now, I'm just Viktor. And who might you be, Miss—"

"Dietrich. Miss Elsa Dietrich," she extends her hand. "I'm on exchange from Hamburg. Or at least I was. I was hoping to study with you this fall ..."

"Ah, Hamburg," Viktor switches to a flawless German. "So, you *are* German, then? My friend Martin thought as much. Not working for them, I hope?" He laughs.

"Polish-German. I spent my summers visiting my grandmother here as a child, but it feels like I'm discovering the city for the first time. Is my Polish accent that bad?" She blushes with embarrassment.

"No, your German is just that good." Viktor winks. "Speaking of, will you be attending Professor

Dawidowicz's talk at the university this afternoon? Classes may be postponed, but they can't stop us from having a conversation."

"Yes, I heard about that … on the barbarity of modernity?"

"The modernity of barbarity, I believe. One and the same. It's all semantics. So … you will come then?"

Elsa blushes in a different kind of way. "Unfortunately, I can't. But it was very nice to meet you, Professor Bauman. Perhaps another time."

"With pleasure. And please, call me Viktor, Miss Dietrich."

"The pleasure is all mine. And thank you again for the saltshaker."

Viktor takes a bow and tips his hat again. "Enjoy your soup. And dare I say, I hope we meet again in more amicable circumstances …"

Viktor returns to his table, where a tall, graceful woman with long brown hair and a lithe, shifty man are bickering. Elsa picks up her pen. *The professor finally spoke to me. He has such a kind smile. His older friend, Martin, doesn't like me. He's always glaring. Rachel and Tadeusz are fighting again …*

"And what happened here?" Rachel points at the coffee stain.

"Take a guess," Martin nods towards Calel.

"Twice in two days … you're next," Tadeusz smiles at Rachel, but she doesn't reciprocate.

Viktor intervenes. "So, how are the children?"

Elsa finds Viktor's attempt at peacemaking endearing.

"The children are fine," Rachel says. "They're at Joel's

apartment for piano lessons."

"Ah, Joel Bronstein," Martin says. "He used to be such a great pianist."

"Don't be an ass," Rachel replies.

Viktor redirects the conversation once again. "And how are Little Tadeusz and Ania's spirits?"

"The sirens don't seem to bother them," Rachel glares at Tadeusz. "Because for *some reason*, Tadeusz has gotten it into their heads that it's all part of a big game!"

"Oh please," Tadeusz replies. "Would you rather I tell them the truth?"

"No, I'd rather you not say this whole thing is a game of hide-and-seek. Squeezing our entire family into your fantastical cabinet won't save us from the bombs. You realize that, right?"

"Where would you rather hide, under the bed?"

"I swear," Rachel shakes her head. "Sometimes I wonder if he acts this way for the children's sake or his own."

"A magical cabinet! I want one," Martin seems amused.

"It's *not* a cabinet," Tadeusz snaps. "It's a custom wardrobe. I've been working on it for months. My mentor says it's one of the best he's ever seen."

"His name's Singer, right?" Martin asks.

"Yes."

"He carved me a chess board—a good man. And by the way, lower your voice," Martin nods in Elsa's direction. "We have listeners."

Elsa returns her gaze to her bowl of potato soup but keeps listening.

"…been obsessed with this for months … " Rachel

whispers. "And the last time he … never-ending fantasy … almost suffocated … caretaker has a contact in a nearby village."

"It isn't a fantasy," Tadeusz raises his voice. "Okay, okay, I'll shut up. But really, Martin, she's not a threat. Anyway, can we not do this here, Rachel? How are *you*, Viktor? How's the treatise coming along?"

"Oh, you know, terribly as always. The German publisher terminated my contract, but that was to be expected. Given the political climate, the French editors have told me the academy might not approve."

"To hell with the academy," Rachel retorts. "You're better off without them. As if publishing were ever the point. Just finish the damn thing so I can read it, Viktor. I mean it. How long has it been, five years? I know a dozen other painters who'd like to read it, too. We need reminders of what is beautiful, now more than ever."

"I'll raise a glass to that," Martin says. "Where'd that boy go off to? How about a round of vodka?"

"No, I have to get back to the children," Rachel replies. "Promise me, the both of you, that you'll consider our offer if things get bad?"

Tadeusz's eyes grow wide. "*Really*, Rachel? You want to have that conversation here? I've told you: my mother's house is out of the question."

"Oh yes," Martin chuckles. "The Great Maternal Jew Hater. She'd be lovely to visit over the holidays."

Rachel ignores Martin. "Just think about it, Viktor."

"Martin, you're incorrigible." Tadeusz hugs Viktor and catches a glimpse of Elsa from across the terrace. "She's taken quite an interest in you..."

Elsa suppresses a smile and turns away.

"Oh, please," she hears Rachel say. Rachel smirks at Elsa as she passes.

"Miss Dietrich? I have a message for you," the clumsy waiter hands Elsa a telegram, which turns the fluttering butterflies in her stomach to dust:

COME TO FIND YOU TWO DAYS AT MOST LOVE CARL

Lieutenant Carl Becker is sitting on a tree stump at the edge of a pine forest. He's come to Poland in the name of the Fatherland, and he's come to sit on this tree stump to write a letter. A chilly autumn breeze shakes pine needles to the forest floor. The pine trees are tall enough to block the midday sun, their dappled shade a welcome change from the singed landscape the *Wehrmacht* has left in its wake. Lieutenant Carl Becker isn't a soldier but a reserve policeman sent to Poland to round up partisans and carry out policing duties behind the front lines. Gunshots ring out from deep within the woods, but Carl doesn't investigate. He prefers to write Elsa another letter he won't send, a letter he'll stuff into his jacket pocket, next to his heart.

According to his grandmother, Carl looks like the ideal Aryan, but he's never felt particularly attractive or comfortable in his own skin. His robust triangular frame suggests the build of a strong swimmer, but Carl moves through the world like a middle-aged fish out of water. His lack of spatial awareness is only the most apparent vestige of his boyish self: his elbows and shoulders bang into corners, and he occasionally hits his forehead on low-hanging door frames too.

swim with you. Can you forgive me?

Carl's mother would take him to the seaside in his home-town in Danzig. It was the only place his father refused to go. He was sitting on the sand as the tide came in, watching the waves crash over her. The current was strong that day, and the water was cold, but she swam anyway. The white noise of the waves used to calm him, until he watched the Baltic Sea swallow his mother alive.

What I want to tell you is that I am sorry. Please understand it is only because I love you. I do not like the idea of you being around other men who admire you. Can you understand that? One day, you will understand. I am your protector, Elsa. You are my duty. This war is a distraction. The battalion is marching. I am returning to you, my dear Elsa.

The sound of twigs snapping and leaves crunching beneath heavy footsteps. He hastily folds the letter and hides it in his shirt pocket as a group of reserve policemen enter the clearing. Some of the more brazen non-commissioned officers have started confiscating love letters; they say it's distracting to think about love during times of war. The most opinionated of Carl's comrades, Lieutenant Cornelius Landau, has been particularly nasty the last few days. Although Cornelius is ten years younger than Carl, he is SS, higher ranking, and highly critical of any wartime sentimentality.

A buzzing fly lands on Carl's sleeve, fidgets, cleans its mouthparts, and flies away. Carl hears the metallic groan of troop transport trucks come to a halt just beyond the clearing and watches four soldiers lead two dozen prisoners into the woods. From this distance, the colors of the Polish uniforms are indistinguishable from their German counterparts. Carl lights a cigarette and turns his back on the situation. He peers through a clearing to gaze at the swirling wheat fields and golden haystacks stretching towards the horizon.

Multiple rifle salvos deep within the forest destroy any semblance of peace or calm. Carl extinguishes his half-smoked cigarette and places it into a small metallic tin, a gift from Elsa.

"You're still using that thing?" Lieutenant Cornelius Landau sits in the grass next to Carl's tree stump. "We're in Poland now, for fuck's sake, just throw it in on the ground."

Carl shakes his head. "The region's being annexed as we speak. This will be Germany soon. Haven't you seen all the *Volksdeutsche* welcoming us in the villages?"

"Oh, I've seen them alright," Cornelius grabs at his crotch. "But they're not exactly *Germans*, are they? You can't be too careful in the land of the *Untermenschen*."

Cornelius snatches Carl's cigarette tin and empties its ashes onto the grass. Carl looks at the pile of dust and does nothing.

"The region is still infected with Jews, you know," Cornelius says. "It hasn't been cleansed yet. And don't get me started on what's further east—that'll be the real job."

"I already told you I'm not going further east," Carl replies. "I'm staying in Łódź with Elsa. Major Brandt promised me some kind of job, too."

Cornelius laughs. "*Promised you some kind of job.* And what do you call *this*? Volunteer work? The real task is here, Carl. You're a German, aren't you? How can you tie yourself down to a woman in a time of war? You said it yourself: the region's being annexed. There's German pussy everywhere. Didn't that bitch leave you anyway? Word of advice, Carl: fuck these *Volksdeutsche* from behind, and preferably in the dark … some of them really *do* look like *Untermenschen*."

Carl feigns a laugh to appease Cornelius, who reaches into his jacket pocket to pull out a tube of white tablets.

"Want one?" Cornelius pops a pill into his mouth.

"No thanks. I want to be clear-headed when I meet Elsa."

"Oh, for fuck's sake. We'll be in Łódź in thirty-six hours. Live a little. This is war, Carl."

"You just wish you had someone waiting for you."

"Ha! *Waiting*!" Cornelius stands over Carl. "I've fucked seven girls in the past five days. What do I need with some cunt waiting for me?"

"She isn't a cunt. I love her. Don't call her that."

"After the way she treated you? That's not how you told it last night."

Cornelius calls out to a teenage reservist walking by. "Hey, you! Come over here and tell Carl about the blonde from the other day."

A baby-faced soldier in oversized fatigues walks up to them from across the clearing. "He's not lying. The man's a machine. The blonde behind the village square yesterday … you should've seen her tits."

"Carl's an ass man, which means he's a queer," Cornelius puts his arm around Carl's shoulder. "He won't even take one of these Stuka pills before we head out. We'll see you later, Carl. We're going to go watch."

Cornelius shoves Carl away, puts his arm around the young recruit and follows a group of SS men leading Polish soldiers into the forest. Carl looks at the pile of ash on the ground and scoops up what he can as another salvo rings out, expelling a squawking flock of birds from the forest canopy. *Déjà vu.*

He takes a sip of vodka from his canteen and returns to the trucks, carefully crossing the grassy clearing by stepping in the imprints of matted grass where others have been.

The convoy chugs through the evening beneath a bruised September sky. There's little resistance left in the razed Polish towns. In one hamlet of no more than ten stone dwellings, an elderly man walks into the road and curses the invaders with shaking fists. An SS man at the front of the truck column jumps out of a black sedan, places the barrel of his pistol against the elder's forehead, and fires. Red mist and brains shimmer like sea spray in the truck beams.

Carl vomits at the sight of it.

Cornelius laughs. "Better get used to it. Welcome to the land of the *Untermenschen.*"

truth

"I rebel: against my past, against history and against a present that places the incomprehensible in the cold storage of history and thus falsifies it in a revolting way."

—Jean Améry, *At the Mind's Limits*, 1966

I realize I lied earlier. The writing on the spine of *The Rise and Fall of the Third Reich* was white, not red. Red made for a better visual, but it wasn't the truth, so lest I make a mistake again, now that other memories are fading, let me repeat the truth: the writing on the book spine was white, not red. The distinction between what is remembered and "the truth" even has its own fancy word amongst academics—historicity.

Another mistake from earlier: I suggested World War Two began on September 1, 1939. At best, this is a half-truth, at least according to a 2009 Telegraph article by Bob Graham. On August 31, 1939, a Polish farmer named Franz Honiok was abducted from his home and murdered on the German-Polish border, thus becoming the first casualty of World War II. According to the facts, Honiok, a sovereign Polish citizen, was killed by known members of the German security services *the night before* Hitler's armies invaded Poland. Honiok was kidnapped, drugged, outfitted in a Polish Army uniform, and executed at the border. The point was to insinuate Poland had attacked Germany first; but to suggest World War Two started on August 31, 1939, changes the official story, and requires an understanding of Operation Himmler, a series of false-flag operations conducted before the "official" beginning of World War Two.

Upon further research, I've learned about the Jabłonków Incident, when the Polish Army repelled German Abwehr agents along the Polish-Slovak border, six days *before* Franz Honiok's murder … but if this was the first German military operation of the war, why don't we speak of August 25, 1939, as the beginning of World War Two?

Alas, it seems all we can ever do is approximate some sense of truth. The writing on the book spine of *The Rise and Fall of the Third Reich* was white, not red, and there is more than one possibility to the beginning of World War Two.

Hear the crickets and their pulsing sounds. The sound of night. The rustle of trees. Men with rifles huddle together beneath a wooden radio tower, black and skeletal; the building grasps for something in the moonlit expanse.

On the road, exposed, reads a signpost: Gleiwitz. The men await the signal: "Grandmother is dead."

Does Franz Honiok squirm? Is he hog-tied on the ground? We know this Polish farmer was abducted from his home in broad daylight on August 31, 1939 … but when they came for him, was he raking, tending to livestock, or feeding the pigs? Did he even have pigs? And would it change the history if he did? Surely Franz Honiok didn't invite his captors inside for tea, but did he peek through the blinds when he heard the truck pulling up? Was it a truck? Or was it a *Volkswagen*? And if Franz Honiok had window curtains, did he hide behind them? Were they white? Were they long, thick, and red?

It is August 31, 1939, and the history books will soon forget Honiok's real name in favor of a German codename: *konserve*, "canned meat." Once attacked, drugged, and cloaked in a Polish Army uniform, Honiok's captors will drag him to the Gleiwitz radio station. *SS-Sturmbannführer* Alfred Naujocks is at the helm of this operation (his affidavit at the Nuremberg Trials says as much), but who are the other commandos alongside him? Are their names important? Why or why not?

What's important tonight is these men are here to justify an invasion. Tonight, both history and language will change irrevocably. Previously innocuous terms are already beginning to take on new meanings: *Polish farmer, canned meat, special task, Gleiwitz,* and hundreds of other words transmogrified to mask the reality of death.

The special unit approaches the sleepy radio station. Under cover of night and the sound of crickets, somebody injects Franz Honiok with poison. He takes his final breath some time before the elite SS unit masquerading as Polish saboteurs dump his corpse like a prop onto the stage of history, filling his cadaver with bullet holes for good measure. A lanky, insectan SS-Major disguised in a Polish uniform is among the first inside. He inserts a pistol into the mouth of a German radio operator, his brethren, and cackles with glee as a man named Karl Hornack—this man really did exist—takes hold of the radio transmitter to tell the first lie of World War Two: "*Uwaga! Tu Gliwice. Rozglosnia znajduje sie w rekach polskich!*" ("Attention! This is Gliwice! The radio station is in Polish hands.") Although the transmission is weak and the Polish accent affected, credibility has never been part of Hitler's *casus belli*.

"Last night, Polish soldiers opened fire for the first time on German soil," Hitler announces just a few hours later. "This morning, Germany retaliated. From now on, bombs will be met with bombs."

Abduct a Polish farmer, change his outfit, deem him canned meat, and dump his costumed body at a radio station. It is all too human how quickly the past succumbs to perception. But what about the Truth? What would Franz Honiok have said? Perhaps that he was more than an anecdote, more than a forgotten casualty of World War Two. Perhaps that history is a fiction first written by the aggressors, only to be revised by the victors and forgotten by the rest.

But what becomes of the vanquished, of those who once lived? History, in the end, is the study of our own deception.

Viktor doesn't want to believe what his colleague and friend, Professor Henryk Dawidowicz, told him yesterday.

"They have a list, Viktor. They'll be coming for us next."

The fear tingles on his bottom lip and whispers to him from the empty streets of his usually bustling, working-class neighborhood of Bałuty. Today is market day. By now, the roads should be filled with tradespeople from all over the region, fabric hawkers with hand carts and horse-drawn carriages shouting at the top of their lungs to sell their wares. Instead, all is quiet beneath Viktor's fifth-story window. The factory bells aren't ringing and Viktor can't hear the low hum of the sewing machines at the tailors across the street.

Viktor peers out of his window. Not a single rug, towel, or garment hangs from a laundry line or billows from the windows of any apartments down below. Could Henryk be right? Is today the day? Henryk's words kept Viktor awake last night.

"Viktor, this is no time for levity. They're targeting the intelligentsia. We must be prepared."

We must be prepared, but how? And prepared for *what*? Viktor closes the window on the silent world below and trips over a pile of books on his way to the kitchen. *Tomorrow*, he recalls an old proverb, *is the busiest day of the week.*

"I have it on good authority that death squads are already sweeping the countryside for Polish elites and academics."

Viktor goes to the sink to fill a rusted tea kettle and places it atop the potbelly stove in the center of his tiny kitchen. He waits for the water to boil at the small round table in the kitchen corner, but his façade of nonchalance is faltering. For the first time since leaving London, Viktor is struggling to maintain his optimism. The cold sore is growing, too.

A dull boom of artillery catches flight on a breeze as the tea kettle begins to screech. Viktor reaches for his favorite mug with the thick blue handle, which Helen used to hold close to her mouth with both hands, smiling and giggling; he can still see her standing at the sanatorium entrance, bewildered and alone.

"Mark my words, Viktor: this won't be like before. It's already being written."

They wouldn't let Helen keep the mug for safety reasons. Viktor hates that memory. He focuses on preparing his tea, just like she taught him: pour the hot water into the mug, add a teaspoon of sugar, and only add a cloud of milk once the water becomes opaque.

"I saw it firsthand. Shmuel only just managed to escape from Złoczew. It was a pogrom. A death squad shot hundreds in the square—and not just Jews, either. They're coming for all of us, Viktor …"

Viktor tongues his tingling bottom lip, wraps his hands around the tea mug, and presses its hot edge to the cold sore. The heat reminds him of how Elsa so delicately spooned her steaming soup at the Astoria. He knows it's juvenile and surely pathetic, but she gave him a possibility worth smiling about, didn't she? And that's something, isn't it?

"Don't shrink your feelings," a mentor once taught Viktor. "Never revert. Always *expand*."

But Henryk's lingering voice invades his thoughts: *"… reports of targeted mass killings; Polish academics, artists, former officers. Ethnic German Poles are participating, too."*

Viktor sits on the edge of his bed with his tea and sips. He knows writing would help—writing anything at all, *to hell with the treatise*—but writing would require clearing off his desk, which would mean deciding which books to keep for research and which papers to throw away.

"… empty your office, Viktor. Destroy what you can. Most of the books we own are a death sentence. And whatever you do, don't let them find your manuscript."

At least Viktor doesn't have to worry about that. There's only one copy, and even he can't find it beneath the hundreds of academic reviews, books, and unpublished papers piled atop his mahogany desk. Tadeusz and Martin helped Viktor salvage his collection from the university, ferrying everything in dozens of oversized wicker baskets from Sasha's bakery. But now, the entire surface area of Viktor's 20m2 apartment resembles the surface of his desk, and he can feel a second cold sore forming on his upper lip, and the anxiety keeps mounting as he smells the familiar wisps of vapor seeping up through the floorboards, courtesy of his downstairs neighbor's rank cabbage stew. He never liked Mrs. Eberhardt or the smell of her cooking, or the vapors' effect on the damp, warped wooden floorboards that now sag beneath the weight of his entire book collection.

Viktor splashes the tepid water from his wash basin on his face and inspects himself in the old mirror he uses for shaving. Out there, everyone expects something of him—a joke, a smile, a word of reassurance—but Viktor is neither a prophet nor a friend, not today. Back in his university days, Viktor published a book of poetry, but the subsequent silence became a source of shame. Since then, he hasn't published much of anything at all … a few articles here and there, but who reads academic journals anyway? Rachel, Tadeusz, and Sasha still call him a writer (Martin put it bluntly: "Viktor, you're faltering"), but for the first time in twenty years, Viktor won't be going back to school in the autumn.

Viktor moves closer to the mirror and covers his face completely, peeking at his reflection as if he were a child playing a game. He wants to catch a glimpse of the Professor Viktor Bauman others see, a man of levity and for whom life comes easily. Carefree. *Ha*. He used to speak to esteemed academics in crowded lecture halls. He used to think it meant something, having a Ph.D. And yes, in a different world, a different life, he might be known for his accomplishments: a master's in history and a Ph.D. from the University of Vienna; an additional master's in psychiatry from Kings College, London; a Distinguished Professorship in History at the Free University in Łódź; and two other honorary degrees from Oxford and the Sorbonne. But what remains of "The Professor" on this day of days? Was it not an illusion all along? Viktor glares at his reflection. What was he trying to prove all those years? What use is philosophy in the face of death squads? What can Voltaire or Mary Shelley say to explain the Luftwaffe strafing columns of refugees outside town?

"My wife and I are fleeing to the countryside tonight. You'd be wise to do the same. Don't be in the city when they come."

The scent of Mrs. Eberhardt's cabbage stew is now wafting up through the floorboards, and Viktor is feeling light-headed. He has to go out, come what may. Martin said he'd be at the Astoria "to witness the spectacle."

Viktor puts on his best suit, ties his shoes, loops a scarf around his neck, and glares back at his crowded studio apartment packed with stacks of papers and towers of books. He shuts the door quietly lest he rouse Mrs. Eberhardt, but she's waiting for him on the landing.

"You made quite a racket this morning, you noisy rat," she croaks. "Why is my ceiling sagging? You'll be paying for that, you know."

"Good morning, Madame," Viktor ignores her and continues down the stairwell.

"Did you hear what I said?" She calls down him. "Your time is coming, professor!"

"Have a nice day, Mrs. Eberhardt!" Viktor shouts back

at her leering face.

Viktor likes starting his day early to avoid the beggars, just before the factory bells rouse the city from its slumber. He's ashamed to admit it, but Viktor always lowers his eyes when he passes the beggars. If he looks at them, he'll have to fake searching his pockets for money he doesn't have to give. At the sleepy Bałut Market, he greets a few vendors who, despite the frequent air raid sirens, have set up their tables to sell their wares. Usually, as soon as the sun is up, the market bursts into a bustling bazaar where people from all over Poland come to search for treasure. Today, however, the market is empty save a few salesmen cornering civilians into tight alleyways, trying to make their daily quota.

A cold wind chases Viktor across the empty marketplace and leads him into the alleyways connecting his neighborhood to the great tree-lined boulevard of Zgierska Street. A man with frenzied eyes barrels into Viktor in a narrow alleyway.

"Agh! Get out of my way!" The man disappears around the corner before two others sprint after him in his wake.

As Viktor emerges from Bałuty's labyrinth onto Zgierska Street, three slow-moving cars honk in unison as they roll down the street. When he finally arrives at the Astoria, a squawking flock of birds startles a young couple as they hastily pay their bill, spilling a tray of coins across the terrace. The couple hurries away without picking up the money. Viktor crouches down to gather the Polish złoty.

"Don't bother. It'll soon be useless," Martin blows a plume of smoke into the air. Viktor picks up the coins anyway and sits at his usual table with Martin and Henryk.

"I thought you were leaving, Henryk," Viktor says.

"He suddenly remembered he had a brain," Martin responds.

"Can you stop exhaling that filth in my face?" Henryk takes off his hat to fan away the cigarette smoke. "My father died with one of those things in his mouth."

"My father died while taking a shit," Martin replies.

"Why do you have to be so crass?" Henryk asks.

"Because the subject demands crassness. Which reminds me, Viktor, I wrote a new joke. You'll like this. A Jew, a queer, and a professor walk into a Nazi bar. What do they order?"

"Don't answer him," Henryk warns.

"Humor me," Martin says.

"Go on. What do they order?" Viktor asks.

"Nothing," Martin grins. "They're taken out back and shot in the head."

Viktor's stomach drops. The faint sound of heavy machinery rumbles in the distance. Viktor notices ripples in Martin's cup of coffee and now the rhythmic sound of marching boots on the wind.

Calel the Waiter arrives out of breath at the table. "What do we do?"

Martin leans back and rubs his belly. "Bring us a few vodkas, won't you?"

"Don't be idiotic," Henryk stands to leave.

"And where are you going exactly?" Martin responds. "We're not going to *run*. Where *exactly* would we go?"

Teacups begin chattering on porcelain saucers. Viktor is at a loss for words. He looks at the empty table where Elsa sat yesterday and picks at his cold sore. A motorcycle and its sidecar speed down the avenue, a Nazi flag billowing in its wake. "Come out, proud Germans! We are your liberators!" The side-car passenger screams.

Another motorcycle roars towards them, and then another, and then one more, and now a stream of black sedans occupied by members of the SS. The groan of killing machines weighs heavy on the land. Two tanks approach, followed by a snaking line of troop transports and panzer wagons as far as Viktor dares to see. Red banners spill out from windows like tongues.

Exhaust fumes from troop transports cloud Viktor's vision. The image of this glorious avenue, once home to the city's most luxurious hotels, bars, and cafés, already seems like a postcard from far away. Soldiers in gunmetal gray greet the hundreds of ethnic Germans now lining the streets, chanting and raising their hands towards the heavens with a crazed look in their eyes. Is it joy? Is it hatred? Each face tells a different story as locals bring bread, flowers, and baskets filled with fruit and vegetables to greet their supposed liberators. Polish-German children climb onto their elders' shoulders to glimpse King Tigers and panzers and artillery trucks and half-tracks and the sleek, black curves of the SS Mercedes-Benzes.

Viktor is now in Nazi Germany, where the *Volksdeutsche* chant in unison and sing songs of victory. Kisses are blown and flowers are thrown. At first, the song is subtle, a garbled, guttural melody, but soon it becomes an affirmation, a warning from all directions: *Deutschland, Deutschland über alles, Über alles in der Welt! Millions are already looking to the swastika, full of hope! The day breaks for freedom and for bread!*

Viktor, Martin, Calel, and Henryk watch as ethnic German locals mutate into a singular, faceless mass, a wild-eyed promise of violence, of rigid raised hands in the air, barking the only words this mob now knows: "*Heil Hitler! Heil Hitler!*" it chants over and over and over again as young soldiers emerge from the torrent of gray vehicles to kiss local women and survey their new surroundings as conquerors.

Without a word, Henryk disappears through the back of the café, and only now does Viktor notice Elsa sitting inside at the bar.

A brief moment of calm before a burly SS officer flanked by two others breaks the momentary spell.

"Who's in charge here?"

Calel approaches, head bowed. In Polish, he asks the officer if he would like a table.

The officer unsheathes his dagger from his waistband. "*Ich spreche nicht die Untermenschen-Sprache.* But of course, you don't speak German, do you, filthy rat?"

Calel doesn't understand.

Viktor intervenes. "*Guten Tag, Herr Offizier.* The boy doesn't speak—"

"Shut your mouth," the SS officer brings his knife's blade to Calel's face. "Kneel, *Untermensch.* I've heard about this cockroach café."

Calel begins pleading as he crouches to the ground. The officer and his underlings roar with laughter as Calel squirms on his knees beneath the officer's blade. The commander grabs Calel by the hair and drags the knife across his forehead. Viktor looks away just as the blood drips down Calel's screaming face.

"Stay where you belong. *Du bist jetzt in Deutschland. Ist das verstanden?*" The commander says as he leaves.

A new fear bubbles in Viktor's belly, pushing bile up his esophagus into the back of his throat. Elsa emerges from the café and runs over to Calel to press a white linen napkin to the gash on his forehead, but Viktor can't stomach the sight of it. He scrambles to the bathroom to vomit. When he returns the terrace is empty save Martin, calmly smoking a cigarette.

"Ah, you just missed it," Martin explains. "A Gestapo man scolded that woman for helping Calel. He even knew her name. Gave her a message. You still think she's on our side?"

Viktor collapses into a chair and stares at the Nazi flags billowing from the windows all along the boulevard.

"Welcome to the Third Reich," Martin says.

Viktor closes his eyes and tries to will away this reality, focusing instead on the lingering scent of Elsa Dietrich's perfume.

It's been three days since Elsa received the telegram, and it's no longer safe to ignore the message:

REPORT FOR DUTY IMMEDIATELY

She walks through the heavy doors of the squat brick building at the corner of Zgierska and Limanowskiego Streets and tells the receptionist there must be a mistake.

"Ah, no, Miss Dietrich. There's no mistake," the bird-faced, tight-haired receptionist smiles curtly. "The major has been asking about you. He'll be with you momentarily."

The receptionist looks over Elsa's outfit and gestures for

her to lean over the half-moon reception desk. "If I were you, I'd remove that scarf and unbutton that top button. SS-Major Brandt can be quite *particular* about his personal assistant's attire."

Elsa recoils and wraps her yellow silk scarf more tightly around her neck. Two SS men walk past and ogle like teenage brutes. "Brandt sure knows how to pick them," one says.

Elsa sits on a hallway bench and crosses her legs. Here in this marble interior with imposing, vaulted ceilings, she can't help but recognize the familiar sense of being trapped.

Elsa was caught swing dancing with her cousin and some friends in Hamburg one year ago. When the Gestapo discovered the illegal dance troupe, they took her and a dozen others to the police department. Her male friends disappeared and the women were jailed in individual cells. On her second day in captivity, a handsome jailer gave her a seemingly simple ultimatum: have dinner with him and be released, or face Gestapo interrogation. One month later, Lieutenant Carl Becker proposed, and although Elsa hardly knew him, it was an opportunity to escape her parents' conservative Nazi household.

The prospect of a happy marriage lasted a few weeks, until Carl's paranoia and jealousy turned violent, destroying any illusion that she could live peacefully with her former jailer. And so, in April 1939, at twenty-one years old, with a black eye and a fractured rib from being pushed down the stairs, Elsa withdrew as much money as was permitted from the family bank account and boarded a train to Poland, the land of her ancestors.

"Miss Dietrich?" The receptionist's voice resonates

across the marble flooring. "This is SS-Major Brandt."

A tall, gaunt man dressed in a black suit glides towards her. His gait is delicate, his voice high and nasal, his face a symmetry of stark shadows.

"Hello, Miss Dietrich. My name is SS-Major Ulrich Brandt. You're even more beautiful than your fiancé mentioned. Please, follow me."

"I don't have a fiancé," Elsa doesn't stand up. "And there must be a mistake. I have no business here."

"No mistake, Miss Dietrich. Follow me. I won't ask again."

Elsa doesn't budge.

"Don't be petulant, Miss Dietrich. Your father would disapprove."

Major Brandt grabs Elsa by the wrist with surprising strength and yanks her through the busy lobby stirring with Nazi officials. The sickly-sweet smell of Brandt's cologne nauseates her, a mixture of leather, cognac, and rotting wood.

Brandt maintains his grip until they're behind his closed office door. "So, Miss Dietrich. From what I understand, you speak quite good Polish. You learned how to speak in secondary school, correct? Please, sit."

SS-Major Brandt looks her over from behind his large desk. Elsa avoids his gaze to survey the room in the dim lighting, its dark brown walls bare save a portrait of Adolf Hitler and a replica of Leonardo da Vinci's Vitruvian Man. The large bay windows behind the desk are shrouded in red curtains. The excess fabric drapes over a spiral staircase's iron railing, which leads to the entrance of a cellar.

"I'm sorry, sir, but there's been a mistake."

"You will address me as *Herr Major Brandt*, Miss Dietrich. Frankly, I am offended you do not remember me. I will not ask again: *sit down*."

"Herr Major Brandt. There's been a mistake. I have no interest in—"

"What, exactly, makes you think I care about your *interests*, Miss Dietrich? You will speak when spoken to. And now it is time for you to listen."

Major Brandt's tight-lipped smile stretches across his face. His desk is covered in graphs, papers, and meticulous lists weighed down by iron paperweights of mythical birds of prey.

"Miss Dietrich," Brandt continues. "You are here because I willed it. You should know by now that there is little point in believing you have control. We have vetted your *dossier* and everything checks out. I need a Polish translator and a reliable typist; lo and behold, you are here. Your fiancé was adamant that you were right for the position. Are you saying he is a liar, Miss Dietrich? Is there something about Lieutenant Becker I should know? Your family seems to think he is good for you, too, and I would hate to see something happen to them, especially your sweet cousin. Ah yes, her stutter is quite endearing, though a lesser educated man might think she's not quite right in the head ..."

Elsa's face grows hot as she begins to make sense of it all. Major Brandt was there in Hamburg. She recognizes his pungent scent.

"Ah, so you do remember me, don't you? Yes, the first time I saw you I knew we would meet again. I, for one, do not believe in coincidences."

Brandt relishes in Elsa's stunned silence.

"Don't act so confused, Miss Dietrich. Did you really think a measly policeman had the authority to release you? Do you think your pitiful fiancé has anything to do with your freedom? Yes, your father is a loyal party member, but it is mostly because of me, Miss Dietrich. The SS has places for those who think they can change the course of history. From what I understand, you've been spending quite a lot of time at the Bolshevik café. You've been writing in a diary, too, haven't you? Hand it over, Miss Dietrich."

"I don't have it with me. There's nothing useful in it anyway."

"I will be the judge of what is and isn't useful. So, let me make this perfectly clear: as my new secretary, you will follow my orders. If you do not follow my orders, you and your idiot cousin will join the rest of your swing-dancing friends outside of Munich. Is that understood, Miss Dietrich?"

Brandt stands up and goes to the curtained window. "Beauty *and* hubris. A fatal combination in my experience. How arrogant you must be to think that this world has been given to you, to think it is yours for the taking and not *you* for *it*?"

Brandt looks at her from over his shoulder. She stares back at him but remains quiet.

"But it doesn't all have to be so serious." Brandt draws the red curtains aside to take a quick peek outside, allowing a sliver of light to slip in.

The thin ray of sunshine cuts like a knife across his wooden desk. "As my personal secretary, your tasks will initially seem quite banal. But do not confuse banality with simplicity, Miss Dietrich. For example, next time, you will bring me that notebook. That is your first task as my new assistant. When the phone rings, you will answer it. Always in German, of course. I will provide a list of names for whom you must transfer the call immediately. If one of them calls, you will not ask any questions. Is that understood? Under no circumstances are you to write down anything they say."

Brandt returns to his desk. "When you transfer a call, you will say, 'One moment please,' and then transfer the line. At meal times—I feed at 8 a.m., 12 p.m., and 6 p.m.—you are to make a pot of piping black coffee and prepare a tray of sliced carrots. The carrots must be no longer than an index finger and no shorter than a thumb. Is that understood? If I request food outside meal times, you will stop everything else and provide. And one more thing, Ms. Dietrich: when you bring me my provisions, you must knock twice before entering. If I do not reply after the second knock, you are to leave the tray outside my door. Finally, as my typist, you will be prompt with your work. I expect any document I provide to be transcribed within the hour. Is that understood?"

Elsa is speechless. She looks for an escape at the back of the room ... perhaps down the black spiral staircase.

"Ah yes," Brandt walks over and taps on the black iron railing. "This is my private cellar. Under no circumstances are you to use it. Have I made myself clear, Miss Dietrich? Your notebook would have served you to write all of this down. Bring it to me tomorrow. An easy first task, is it not?"

Elsa's mind is blank and her body is numb.

"And one more thing," Brandt comes around to Elsa's side of the desk, bends down, and speaks directly into her ear. "Regarding your work attire here at the Gestapo, you would be wise to heed whatever Frau Wolfmann says. Scarves like this are not to be worn inside."

Brandt uncoils the yellow scarf from Elsa's neck and lets it float to the floor. "I would think a pretty girl like you would want to show off her figure. Goodbye, for now, Miss Dietrich."

It's been a long day of marching and drinking, and Carl's face is red and tight from the sun. He needs to find Elsa but he's got a double shift guarding Freedom Square, where hundreds of ethnic Germans are coming to celebrate their conquerors.

Carl lights a cigarette and leans up against a wall, stares up at the hallmark statue in Freedom Square, and wonders who the hero is.

Cornelius Landau approaches. "Let's go find some women, there's enough men here to do the job."

"I need to get to Elsa. She's staying at the Grand Hotel but she isn't picking up."

"Didn't you say she's working for Major Brandt?" Cornelius opens his fly and begins pissing against the wall. The stench is formidable. "They're probably at the victory ball as we speak."

The thought of Elsa in a tight dress on the arm of an SS officer makes Carl wince.

"What's wrong, fräulein? Never seen a German cock before?" Cornelius mashes his shriveled manhood back into his pants as a woman passes.

"Watch *this*," Cornelius tells Carl and grabs the woman by the wrist. "Look at me when I'm speaking to you,

Untermensch."

"I'm Polish!" The woman says with pride in perfect German.

Cornelius' face twitches. "What's your name? Where do you live?"

"Let her go," Carl intervenes. "She hasn't done anything."

"Not yet. This is our job," Cornelius twists the woman's wrist and pulls his truncheon from his belt. "She's just the type to take a shot at us when we're not looking. Why do you speak German so well?"

Carl pulls Cornelius off of her. "It's not worth it. Officers are watching. Let's get out of here. I need a drink."

As the woman runs away she screams, "The spirit of Kościuszko lives!"

Carl and Cornelius exit Freedom Square and pass a massive bonfire of books and documents and paintings and debris. Embers pop and sizzle as their sparks float up into the darkness. Carl and Cornelius' shadows take on gargantuan size against the illuminated buildings as they make their way into a crowded bar of drunken soldiers.

Carl turns to the elder sitting next to him at the bar. "Who is the statue of in Freedom Square?"

"A ghost," the old man stares down into his drink.

"Yes, I know he's *dead*. But who was he? What did he *do*?"

"Ask the Americans. Ask the Lithuanians. Ask the Poles."

"But I'm asking *you*."

The elder gives Carl a black-toothed smile. "I know better than to talk to your lot about Tadeusz Kościuszko. Now, he's only a ghost, forgotten by history. They're probably tearing him down as we speak."

"Kosey—usko. I know who he was," Carl lies. He shoots back a glass of vodka and stumbles off his barstool.

The world starts spinning as he wades through the crowded bar. He has to find Elsa but Cornelius pulls him back into a headlock and yet another drunken conversation, and soon Carl finds himself singing proud songs of victory alongside drunken soldiers.

Deutschland, Deutschland über alles, Über alles in der Welt.

After the next round of shots, Carl's world goes black.

The faint scent of orange blossom perfume brings him back from the abyss. Somehow, Carl's lizard brain has guided him through the city to the Grand Hotel. He finds himself standing in an elegant corridor, banging on a door with a swollen fist.

Elsa is caught in a nightmare of an unbearably crowded dance hall. She dances the waltz even though "Stompin' at the Savoy" is playing, and although she can feel two hands on her side, she feels terribly alone. Dozens of Gestapo men are standing with their backs to the wall, leering at her while they smoke cigarettes. Somewhere in the distance, a ringing phone cuts through the music, morphing into a pounding on the dance hall door.

Elsa wakes up with a jolt to the silhouette of a large man looming at her bedroom's threshold. She knows better than to scream; she speaks calmly and clearly.

"Hello, sir. You are in the wrong room. My name is Elsa Dietrich. This is my hotel room. Please leave."

The shadowy male figure does not move, only mumbles something into the darkness. Elsa pulls the covers up to her neck. She can smell his stench of cigarettes, urine, and hard liquor. Elsa reaches for the bedside table lamp and pulls the golden chain, illuminating the room in an orange glow.

"Carl?"

"Elsa, my darling!" Carl stumbles into the room. His face is flush and his smile is crooked. He takes a step towards her and grimaces when he recognizes her fear. "I won't hurt you. I promise. I didn't mean to scare you, my darling."

Elsa tucks her knees up to her chest and presses herself against the headboard. Carl settles at the foot of the bed.

"Carl, you're scaring me. Please get out of my room."

He shakes his head. "I tried calling and knocking. Didn't you hear me pounding on the door? I thought you knew I was coming. You could've picked up the phone, you know."

"Knew you were coming? How could I—" Elsa catches herself before raising her voice. She's been here before and she knows how it ends. Elsa speaks to Carl as if backing away from a rabid dog. "Carl, I know you didn't mean to scare me, but it's three in the morning. Please leave my room."

Carl reaches for Elsa's feet. She kicks him away.

Carl stands and begins pacing around the room. "I was given a double shift, okay? It's not my fault. You know I won't hurt you again, darling. I'm here to protect you. But you should have answered the phone. You know I don't like being stood up."

Carl approaches her bedside. Elsa pulls the covers up to her neck.

He backs away. "I—I'm an idiot. I'm sorry. I just thought—well, I'll let you sleep. Perhaps we'll have coffee in the morning?"

Elsa nods to appease him.

"Good. Yes. I'll call you tomorrow," Carl stumbles out of the room.

Elsa waits for the door to close before pushing a desk chair against the door handle. She calls reception and reminds the concierge that she is a secretary to the SS. "If you ever give someone a key to my room again, I'll have you arrested."

Elsa's stomach is in knots. *Of course* Carl found her. She thought moving eight hundred kilometers away would be enough.

The next morning, Elsa lets the phone ring five times before picking up in a fury. "What did I tell you last night? I don't want to speak to you!"

"I a-p-apologize, Miss Dietrich," the young concierge stutters. "But It's Herr Major Brandt. He demands I put him through."

Major Brandt's voice slithers through the receiver and into Elsa's ear. "I didn't think you were stupid enough to ignore my calls. You have precisely twenty minutes to get to the office and bring that little diary of yours, too."

fiction

"We live entirely, especially if we are writers, by the imposition of a narrative line upon disparate images, by the "ideas" with which we have learned to freeze the shifting phantasmagoria which is our actual experience. Or at least we do for a while. I am talking here about a time when I began to doubt the premises of all the stories I had ever told myself, a common condition but one I found troubling."

—Joan Didion, *The White Album*, 1979

My childhood home sold in a matter of days. A family of four was keen to make new memories. They gutted the living room and turned the old bookshelves into an entertainment center.

A few months later, we went to my mother's storage unit in search of old books. I'd been struggling with this story for over a year at that point—struggling to make sense of Viktor, Elsa, and Carl's connection. Armed with a flashlight, I sat in the cramped storage unit and scanned through old textbooks, historical novels, and academic essays in search of the truth I'd known as a boy. What did I need to remember?

My mother was sifting through a box of old trinkets and toys. She asked me if I'd come across any ceramic figurines, specifically a colorful elephant she'd bought me at the zoo. Frustrated that I wasn't finding what I was looking for, I snapped at my mother and reminded her that we'd already boxed up the ceramics and donated them to a thrift store. I turned away from her and began flipping through my tattered copy of *The Rise and Fall of the Third Reich*. Agitated, my mother suggested that what I was searching for couldn't be found in someone else's book.

This annoyed me. In that moment, I didn't want to understand. Instead, I shifted my focus to an old cardboard box filled with some of the first stories, poems, and essays I'd ever written, including the fictional diary of a German soldier in World War One. In the name of authenticity, I'd even soaked its pages in black tea, singed their corners, and bound the whole volume with tattered yarn. The diary was written from the perspective of a young teenager who had no interest in firing his weapon but ultimately went over the top and disappeared into No Man's Land.

I put the diary aside and continued leafing through other documents until I came across a yellowing stack of papers: a short story called "The Lady in the Red Dress." It was a ghost story about a woman who haunted the top of the stairwell in my childhood home. Although she was a ghost, she wasn't pale or bloody or spectral or dismembered, just a young, mysterious lady forever stuck in that liminal space, waiting for somebody to ask why she was there. I took the "Lady in the Red Dress" with me when we left.

On the drive home, my mother took a right turn when she should've taken a left on a route she'd been driving since I was a child.

"How could you forget the way home?" I was incredulous. I knew it was a cruel thing to say, but her aloofness frustrated me, and our last few days together left me concerned about her memory. When I said goodbye to her at the airport, I sensed a growing distance between us.

Armed with the stories from my youth, I spent the months rewriting a story I was only beginning to understand, but the truth of the woman in the red dress remained unclear. The more I tried to invent her, the faster she faded away, and the more I looked for her in history books, the less real she became. I should've listened to my mother: whatever I was searching for wasn't about inventing something new. There was something I still needed to remember. Each fact I investigated about upper-class life in Hamburg in 1939 led to a dozen other possibilities. It was overwhelming. Was the *Swingjugend* in Hamburg really that important to my story? What about the White Rose resistance group that formed in Munich in 1942? Or the various ways in which "racially pure" German women were encouraged to give birth to "Aryan" children in the state-sponsored *Lebensborn* program? It was all too much, and it was never enough, all of the colons, semi-colons, and ellipses of history … how much did I have to learn before remembering my own truth?

It was time to ascend the haunted stairwell and ask the Lady in the Red Dress the right questions.

Acquaintances no longer exchange smiles when they pass, and more and more familiar faces disappear every day. Neighborhood children he's watched grow up avert their eyes. They stay close to their mothers, and Viktor doesn't blame them—he is also afraid.

Just a few weeks into the occupation, Viktor no longer recognizes the city. Street names have changed—~~Freedom Square~~ *Deutschlandplatz*; ~~Piotrkowska Street~~ *Adolf-Hitler-Straße*; ~~Kościuszko-Alee~~ *Herman-Göring-Straße*—and are choked by checkpoints. Viktor has known this kind of emptiness just once before, during the Great Influenza Outbreak of 1918, but here in Łódź, the fear has taken on a different shape: the rhythmic sound of patrolling boots reverberating on cobblestone; café terraces full of jet-black uniforms of the Death's Head; the echoes of rifle salvos and machine gun patter outside of town.

Off the market square in Bałuty, Viktor watches a man deliberately let his dog shit in front of the tailor shop. The store owner comes out with a broom and politely asks the mutt's owner if he'd mind cleaning up the mess.

"I don't have to take orders from you." The dog owner spits at the tailor, who uses his broom to flick the shit back at the dog owner; he flies into a rage and screams at the top of his lungs, "Help! A Jew is attacking me! Police!"

Viktor doesn't linger. He returns to his building quietly to avoid alerting his downstairs neighbor, Mrs. Eberhardt. Emboldened by the occupation, she's found endless new reasons to complain: Viktor makes too much noise too early in the morning; his friends speak too loudly; they all stomp down the stairs; Viktor has stopped having Martin and Henryk over for drinks.

Tonight, he sits at his desk with a pot of tea and listens to the world outside his window. Since the curfew was instated, German voices have been ever-present around Bałut Market and its surrounding alleyways. The Gestapo building on Zgierska Street is around the corner, where, just last week, the SS stopped Viktor and ordered him to be home by 7 P.M. Earlier this week, the curfew changed to 6 P.M., and yesterday he was told to be home by 5:30 P.M. Tonight, as Viktor waits for darkness to fall, he watches the searchlights scan the clear skies for what he hopes could be French and British airplanes.

A purring car in the street below. Viktor recognizes the tailor from earlier throw two suitcases into the trunk of the small car before embracing a stout woman at the curb and rolling away, headlights off.

Not a minute later, a troop transport arrives. Two German policemen bash down the tailor's door.

Simultaneously, a loud bang comes at Viktor's own door and screaming begins below.

"Yes, who is it?" Viktor doesn't open.

"Open the door, Bauman."

Viktor recognizes the unfriendly voice, cracks the door, and tries to summon his usual sense of humor. "Mrs. Eberhardt. It's a bit late for a drink ..."

"Idiot Jew. I am here to inspect your apartment."

She barges in with the stench of fried cabbage in her wake. Her body is frail, her pale arms purple and varicose. She doesn't even glance at Viktor as she begins snooping around his apartment, armed with a pencil and clipboard.

Viktor shadows Mrs. Eberhardt in defiant silence as she invades his privacy, room by room.

"There isn't any silver in there if that's what you're looking for, Mrs. Eberhardt."

"Rubbish. All rubbish," she sifts through the utensil

drawer. "I don't know what I expected to find in this hovel."

Viktor laughs. "Well, you aren't the first woman to insult my taste in cutlery, Mrs. Eberhardt."

She glides past him into the living room. Viktor has an urge to stick out his foot. *I could break her so easily, the haggard witch.* His anger rises as she crouches by his bookshelf to inspect the titles, pulling out one book, tossing another to the floor, sometimes pausing to stroke a book's spine, almost caressing it.

Viktor knows he can't reason with her so he resorts to sarcasm.

"Your husband must be awake with all the racket you're making. Will he be joining us for a cup of tea, too?"

"Freud ... Wilhelm Reich ... Karl Marx," she shakes her head. "Do you really think you'll get away with this, Bauman? These are *illegal*."

Viktor maintains his sarcasm. "I appreciate your concern, madame. I'll burn them in the stove first thing tomorrow!"

Mrs. Eberhardt says nothing. She walks over to the kitchen sink, turns it on to check the water pressure with her pruned finger, and leaves the water running as she steps onto a stool to look through his empty pantry. The blue veins in her hands look like spider webs. Viktor has an urge to send her tumbling to the floor. As a psychiatrist in London, he specialized in patients with dementia. *The scalpel was only ever used as a last resort.* Mrs. Eberhardt looks down at him from the height of the stool, a haunted look in her eyes of misplaced rage.

For an instant, Viktor thinks of Helen. "Mrs. Eberhardt," he calmly steps towards her, holding his hands out in supplication. "I don't want any trouble. But I need you to leave. *Now.* If you would like to make a list of what is to be requisitioned, I think you've seen more than enough. You are trespassing in my home."

Mrs. Eberhardt descends, straightens her brittle back, lifts her pointy chin, purses her thin, dry lips, and scribbles a few notes onto her clipboard.

"Mrs. Eberhardt…" Viktor says through a clenched jaw as he takes a stern step towards her.

"I am a registered *Volksdeutsche*, and you will not raise your voice at me!" She points her pencil at him with each word. "This apartment now belongs to the Reich, and I have a legal right to take stock of all valuables in *Untermenschen* apartments—*half-breeds* included."

Viktor has had enough. He grabs her by the waist and yanks her to the door.

"Help!" She squirms. "Get your hands off me, you monster!"

Viktor deposits her on the landing and holds tight onto her wrist. "Now you listen to me." There is hatred in his voice. "If you ever bother me again, I'll pay a visit to the authorities and tell them *exactly* where you and your husband come from."

Mrs. Eberhardt's face goes white.

"You're not the only one with secrets, you conniving witch." Viktor hears multiple doors opening in the stairwell; he hisses into her ear lest someone hear him. Viktor's words come from somewhere else, from somewhere uncanny.

"How long do you think it will take them to discover you only became German *after* the war? And what about your husband, lying about being a war veteran? If there's one thing they hate more than *my kind*, it's gypsies."

Mrs. Eberhardt writhes and meows in exaggerated pain as she tries to escape Viktor's grip, but something intoxicating and infectious has overcome him—a dreaded fury he's only ever read about in books. He wants to wrap his hands around her neck and squeeze the life out of her. The thought terrifies him. Viktor pulls back his fist and at the last moment, punches the wall instead of Mrs. Eberhardt's horrified face.

She falls back towards the stairwell just as a neighbor arrives to catch her in his arms. "He was going to kill me! The Jew was going to kill me!" Her screeches reverberate throughout the building. Viktor slams his door, locks it before the neighbor can come for him, and rushes to the window for fresh air. A shiver of horror courses up his spine. *What am I becoming? I have to find a way out.*

On the other side of town, Elsa plops a fizzing tablet into a tall glass of water. Given the circumstances, pharmaceuticals are now her best chance at escape. In retrospect, she doesn't know what she was thinking, boarding a train back to Hamburg. She knew there'd be checkpoints throughout the now annexed *Reichsgau Wartheland*, but she didn't realize Brandt's men had been following her. They dragged her off the train in Kutno and brought her back to the Gestapo office, where she spent three nights and two days in Brandt's cellar without food, water, or natural light.

SS-Major Brandt visited her on the third day and brought her a lavish breakfast: freshly baked bread, juice, sausage, eggs, and pastries. Brandt seemed to take great pleasure watching her eat like an animal, soaking up the egg yolk with the still-warm bread, waiting for her to finish before announcing his ultimatum: "If you try to flee again, I will personally escort you to the women's camp on the river Havel. Is that understood? Clean yourself up and report for duty tomorrow. From now on, you will work seven days a week. And now, I have a gift for you," Brandt placed a bottle of orange blossom perfume on the table, the same brand Elsa wears. "These British perfumes aren't easy to acquire these days. Wear it when you come in."

Elsa finishes her glass of fizzing water and feels the reviving effects immediately. She can still see the impact of her captivity in the bags under her eyes, can feel it in the sting of her gnawed cuticles and mangled fingernails, and can hear it gurgling in her gut. She has no appetite, only the desire to drink strong liquor and sleep through the mornings.

Brandt enters the office and jingles his keys playfully. "Today is going to be a good day. Why isn't the coffee ready yet? There's much to discuss."

Elsa holds her skirt down as she rises from her chair and goes to the kitchenette to prepare the coffee. She hocks a wad of white phlegm into the percolator's boiling liquid before going to the medicine cabinet to add to the concoction. She's already experimented with crushing sleeping pills into Brandt's coffee—barbiturates, too—but nothing seems to curb Brandt's frenzied enthusiasm for transforming Łódź into a Nazi city. Elsa spits a second gob into the brew. There are hints of red and green specks in the mucus; currently, this is the extent of her rebellion.

Elsa carries the tray of coffee and sliced carrots through

Brandt's open door to find him standing at the open window, peering up at the stone Church of the Virgin Mary, its steeple towering over the conquered city.

A ray of sun stretches across the carpeted floor. Its light catches dust particles dancing in the sunbeam like snowflakes. For an instant, in Brandt's profile—is it a trick of the light?—Elsa sees a genuine smile before a shadow contorts his face. Is he reciting a song? Or perhaps an incantation under his breath? Brandt stares up at the church steeple and tenderly kisses a piece of jewelry before returning it to his pocket.

"Ah, Miss Dietrich. Please sit down. The security services demand that I keep you in the dark, but look at this."

Brandt splays out a map of the entire world on his desk. "After all, if you are going to be my secretary, you must be privy to certain information. Once England has been conquered, we gain access to the British merchant fleet. And this—ingenious, isn't it?—is when we can begin deporting the Jews *here*," Brandt jabs his index finger at a small piece of land in the Indian Ocean and explains Hitler's plan to deport Europe's Jews to Madagascar. Elsa has heard a lot of fantastical ideas, but this one seems particularly farfetched ... then again, so was Hindenburg ceding power to Hitler in 1933, and the *Reichstag* Fire and the subsequent decrees, and what about the 1935 Nuremberg Laws and the *Mischling* test, not to mention the *Luftwaffe's* terror bombings in Spain, Hitler's annexation of the Sudetenland and Austria, Hitler's alliance with Stalin, his sworn ideological enemy, and now the splitting of Poland in two.

Once upon a time, it all seemed so far-fetched.

"It is going to be a hectic winter, Miss Dietrich," Brandt

finally takes a sip of Elsa's brew. "But let's focus on a more pressing concern: I've been reading through your diary and there's a lot of drivel, but what, specifically, do you know about Professor Viktor Bauman?"

Elsa's stomach tightens. She's written more than a few romantic thoughts about Viktor. Brandt picks up on her unease.

"Not to worry," Brandt smiles. "The intellectual ones are cunning. You wouldn't be the first to be manipulated by their ways. But your description is not a profile, Miss Dietrich. *Kind, handsome, and thirty-something* are simply adjectives. How many times have you spoken to Professor Bauman?"

"Only a few times at the café," Elsa says nervously. "I don't know much about him. Only that he speaks fluent German and used to live in London."

Brandt flips through a few more pages. "Did you know that I used to be a professor, too? Of the racial sciences, in Berlin. I even won an award for my research in Africa."

Brandt pauses in hopes of a response but Elsa remains silent. Brandt continues. "Now that you are my informant, you must learn to record *useful* information. What do I care about the kinds of pastries this half-breed ordered at the bakery? And why are there two pages devoted to his friendship with Martin Arendt? Arendt is a homosexual— an asocial—Miss Dietrich. Are you saying Bauman is too? Now, *that* would be of interest. They are some of the most devious enemies I have ever encountered."

Brandt takes a large sip of his tainted coffee. "Anyway. I've been tasked to arrange a council of prominent Jewish community members, and I'd like you to find out more about this Professor Bauman. What is his background? What exactly did he do in London? A German speaker on the Jewish council will be essential for what's ahead."

"But Bauman is not Jewish, Herr Brandt. Unless I'm mistaken, he is—"

"Do not speak of things you do not understand," Brandt snaps. "He might not be religious, Miss Dietrich, but he is a *Mischling* nonetheless. All the better to sow internal conflict in the council when necessary."

Brandt stands up and walks over to a freshly polished gramophone beneath the portrait of Adolf Hitler. "Before I dismiss you, I'd like you to listen to something, Miss Dietrich."

Brandt is careful with the record player's needle, almost tender. As soon as the song's first chords scratch into being, Elsa recognizes Scott Joplin's "Maple Leaf Rag."

"Do you know what this is?" Brandt asks her with glee.

"Maple Leaf Rag."

"Wrong. It is the devil's work. It's witchcraft. You should know, of course, having fallen victim to such music."

Elsa remembers the joy she felt that first night when her cousin took her dancing in Hamburg. That was the night she met Walter, a swing dancer from St. Louis, who showed her the first steps of the Charleston. A world away.

"Make no mistake, Miss Dietrich, what we are doing here is nothing short of destiny. The key to victory, although some of my colleagues disagree with me, is understanding the black magic of our enemies—be it here, in the *Reichsgau Wartheland*, the Americas, or in Africa."

Elsa has been sitting through similar diatribes for weeks. Already, she feels herself becoming numb to such vile pronouncements.

"There's much to learn in the Americas," Brandt says. "The conquering of the natives, Jim Crow laws, an institutionalized racial order. *All men are created equal*—how glorious! How preposterous! How positively *devious*! To delude an entire people into such myths and fantasies! Which brings me to the question, Miss Dietrich: how did the Americans achieve this grand delusion?"

Elsa knows better than to speak. Brandt never allows her to respond to his constant barrage of rhetorical questions. "It is a simple question of repetition, Miss Dietrich. The Americans are exceptional because they *believe* they are exceptional. They believe this because it is repeated over and over again. Despite centuries of state-sponsored subjugation, ask any American, and they still believe they are the greatest, most ethical people on earth! It has become their collective delusion and so their *moral* conclusion. And *this* is why jazz music is so devious."

Brandt finishes the rest of his coffee in one gulp. Elsa smirks at the thought of her infected mucus sliding down into Brandt's belly.

Brandt coughs to clear his throat. "We cannot conquer our enemies unless we understand their techniques, which is why I'd like you to go to the university library and bring me the works of Professor Samuel Borowski, an anthropologist of the Dark Continent who has worked with Professor Bauman in the past. Borowski is now in hiding, and I intend to find him. It will be a fascinating interrogation, no doubt. After, I will speak to this Bauman character."

"Yes, Herr Brandt. I'll get on it straight away."

"Oh, and one more thing, Miss Dietrich. Many lavish

apartments will be made available for Gestapo employees by the beginning of winter. I'll make sure you have a room with a view of *Adolf-Hitler-Straße*. We'll practically be neighbors."

The Astoria's terrace is a puzzling scene of abandon. Earlier this morning, Viktor received an urgent phone call from Tadeusz: something has happened to Martin.

The early morning fog is just beginning to lift as Viktor arrives on the deserted terrace. Half-smoked cigarettes and warm embers litter the cobblestone; clumps of dark hair are strewn across white linen tablecloths, and shattered crystal shimmers on the ground. Fragments of serving plates crunch beneath Viktor's feet as he approaches the café entrance and calls out to Calel, Martin, and the Astoria's owner, Tomasz Surguine.

Viktor catches movement at the back of the café, where bullets have shattered the restaurant's central chandelier, covering the ground in spent bullet casings. Viktor peeks into the kitchen at a steaming pot of soup and calls out again for Tomasz, but his voice only echoes off the metallic surfaces.

Back in the dining room, Viktor takes a seat at the bar and hears the sound of multiple match strikes. He turns towards the sound to see a tiny glowing ember in the corner of the room.

Viktor approaches cautiously. "Calel, what happened?"

Calel stares straight ahead with bloodshot eyes, his face flush, his lip busted. He inhales ferociously. The burning tip of the cigarette is too close to Calel's trembling fingers.

"What happened?" Viktor repeats softly as ash falls onto Calel's apron.

Tomasz Surguine barges through the café's front door, stinking of vodka and sweat. "Ah, Bauman, you just missed it! They roughed everyone up nice and good. Well, everyone that showed face. Henryk and Martin are cleaning themselves out back."

"What. Happened, Calel?" Viktor keeps his focus on the boy.

"There's no use," Tomasz says. "He's been frozen stupid since they left."

"Since who left?"

"Who do you think, *Professor*? A group of armed Germans came in and shot up the place, asked everyone on the terrace for identification. They also taught a few patrons the meaning of the word butchery." Tomasz points to the bloodstains at the entrance. "Hey kid, snap out of it!" He whaps Calel on the back of the head. "Bauman's here. Get it together. We have to clean up before they come back."

"Leave him be, Tomasz."

"*Leave him be*? The terrace isn't going to clean itself! He got off easy. You should see the others. That's the problem with this generation: they don't know what it's like to live with war. Unfortunately for you, Bauman, you're going to have to leave before they come back. No Jews allowed. You understand."

Tomasz goes behind the bar to fetch a broom and a dustbin. Viktor helps Calel stand up. "Let's get some fresh air on the terrace."

Calel fumbles in his chest pocket for another cigarette.

The cigarette falls limp in his mouth when he finally speaks. "They came in an unmarked truck. They weren't dressed like soldiers. They fired at the chandelier and into the ceiling. They asked for the reservation booklet and the names of everyone on the terrace. They threatened Mr. and Mrs. Perechodnik with a knife. They singled out all the Jewish men with beards. They dragged Henryk into the street. Made everyone watch. That SS officer from the other day was back with his knife."

Calel stares out into the street and takes a long drag. "Henryk was smart. He didn't try to run. One man tried to break free. I could hear it, Viktor. They broke his leg right there on the curb. Mr. Perechodnik made it a bit further before they caught up with him. He didn't even scream, Viktor. He just opened his mouth when they started ..."

Calel's voice disintegrates into a whisper.

"So, you got him talking! Let it out, boy. That's it." Tomasz squeezes the back of Calel's neck and hands him a glass. "Have a sip, boy. It'll do you good. If they're smart, they'll kill Perechodnik and the others outside the city. I've heard they're already digging trenches in the Lagiewnicki woods. The university's being liquidated. Maybe you'll get your job back, Bauman! You speak German, don't you?"

"Just shut up and make yourself useful and get us some water, will you?" Viktor snaps. "The boy doesn't need any vodka. It's not even ten yet."

"Ha! Don't blame the messenger. I'm trying to help. Trust me, the faster we get used to days like this the better. You should've seen the blade they used, Bauman. I've never seen such a clean cut. The whole ear! It was surgical, really."

Calel whimpers and drains the glass of vodka in one gulp.

"See? He likes it," Tomasz gives Calel a playful wallop on the back.

"What surprised me most," Tomasz continues pensively as he lights his own cigarette. "Is that he didn't even scream when they started cutting, not even after they showed him his own ear! You should've seen the hole, Viktor. Like you could almost look inside his head."

The image causes Viktor's vision to flicker. He stands up to confront Tomasz but tips back into his seat. Viktor tries to steady himself by grabbing the table's edge, but suddenly Tomasz's voice sounds impossibly far away.

Viktor's head falls heavy and a high-pitched ringing swipes the earth out from under his feet.

A calming, ethereal voice speaks to Viktor from above. He has a vision of himself and a lover sitting on a park bench in London. She isn't Helen, but she reminds him of her—the gentler parts, anyway. He can hear children playing on the green, a quiet wind and the rustling of leaves and a crackling fireplace. The voice continues to call out to him until he's back on the cobblestone terrace.

His eyes adjust to a searing light and a canopy of familiar faces—Calel, Tomasz, and Elsa Dietrich.

"Professor, let me help you," Calel raises Viktor by the armpits, pulls him into a chair, and hands him a glass of water.

"Breathe. Slowly," Elsa places her hand on Viktor's shoulder. In this moment, her touch is everything. "Drink. Slowly," she says.

The cold water restores his senses. "How long was I out?"

"Only a few seconds," Calel says. "No, stay seated. Don't look at the blood. You took a hard fall, Professor. Miss Dietrich has gone to fetch a towel."

Viktor touches his nose and teeth, relieved to find everything in its right place. Suddenly, only one thought is essential. *She must think I'm an idiot, passing out like this.* "Good morning, Miss Dietrich. So, you witnessed the spectacle?"

Elsa sits down next to him and presses the towel to his forehead. "Don't speak. Just keep that there, Viktor."

The smell of her is enchanting and her gentle hands remind him of elsewhere, of living in the body instead of the mind, of being cared for—of tenderness. Color shimmers back into Viktor's vision with each word Elsa speaks. All of it sounds beautiful to him, no matter that it doesn't make any sense amidst the devastation. Here on the destroyed terrace, Viktor chooses instead to notice the café's golden trim, the vanilla linen tablecloths, the patches of blue sky peeking out from the clouds, and Elsa's red lips.

"Viktor, do you know what day it is?"

"It feels like a Tuesday."

"Where are we, professor?" Her voice becomes stern. "Do you remember who I am?"

"Elsa. Miss Dietrich. Thank you. I'm fine, really. I have these fainting spells on occasion."

"You're not fine, Viktor," Elsa inspects his forehead. "You're as pale as a ghost. You might need stitches."

The thought of stitching a head wound nauseates him, which is why Viktor is happy to let Elsa take his head in her hands and do with him what she will. Elsa keeps the towel pressed to him as she inspects the rest of his injuries. He relishes the exotic scent of orange blossom perfume and her red lips hovering oh-so-close to his forehead.

"What the hell is *she* doing here?" Martin's voice booms and the moment is gone. Elsa recoils at the sight of Martin's bloody shirt and at Henryk, who's pressing a blood-soaked napkin to his face.

"You're not welcome here, woman," Martin spits at Elsa. "What do you care about him? This is your doing, you nasty bitch."

"What the hell is wrong with you!" Viktor stands up to face Martin before losing his balance.

"It's fine, Viktor," Elsa says. "I was just leaving anyway. Keep pressure on the wound. Take care of him. He might need stitches. See you soon, Viktor." Elsa disappears down the boulevard.

"What did you do?" Viktor curses Martin. "She was trying to help!"

"Sit down, you fool. She's working for them. Yes, I have proof. I saw her coming out of the Gestapo building last week."

"That doesn't *prove* anything," Viktor sees the deep wound on Martin's forearm and looks away, only to see the gashes across Henryk's face, which Calel is dabbing at with a wet towel, and only now does Viktor realize the clumps of hair on the terrace may very well be the bloody remnants of Henryk's beard.

"Another millimeter and I wouldn't be here," Henryk keeps the napkin pressed firmly to his neck. "God was looking out for all of us today."

"God!" Martin hollers. "Yes, Henryk. God was with

us today. It really is the best of all possible worlds, isn't it?"

Calel arrives with another bottle of vodka to help disinfect their wounds. Martin sloshes the vodka onto his forearm without so much as a grimace before taking a long swig and handing it to Henryk.

"*L'chaim!*" Henryk raises the bottle.

"To survival!" Martin responds.

Henryk turns to Viktor. "Listen. We have to act quickly. They're going to be back soon. A few hours at most. We have to choose wisely."

"What are you talking about?" Viktor asks.

"It's ingenious, really," Martin interrupts. "They're establishing a Council of Jewish Elders. They came here looking for you. They even know your name. They called you The Half-Breed Austrian. Quite a clever strategy, making the prisoner tie his own noose.

"That's not what's going on, you fool," Henryk disagrees. "They want us to run things ourselves. They know about the pre-war community leadership—social services, welfare, and so on—and this way they can leave us be, Viktor."

"*Leave us be,*" Martin bellows. "Yes, that makes a whole lot of sense. The Nazis want *to leave us be* by making us responsible for our own imprisonment. Sure. And your mangled face was just a free visit to the barber."

Henryk ignores Martin. "Most of the faculty have been detained, Viktor. We have to react before it's too late."

"Why didn't they arrest you?" Viktor asks.

"Because he agreed to collaborate," Martin sneers.

"You ingrate!" Henryk is indignant. "It isn't *collaboration*.

You don't know what you're talking about. The council will be an extension of the Kehilla. They want to keep us at arm's length, and frankly, I prefer it that way. It's not like I have much of a choice, is it? Next time they'll slit my throat. We have to comply."

"This is absurd," Martin replies. "Maybe Henryk can get you a date with that Nazi bitch, Viktor. Let me remind both of you of the kind of people we're dealing with."

Martin unbuttons his bloodstained shirt to reveal a shiny white scar slashed across his belly. "One of the many souvenirs of *compliance* in Dachau. Or would you like to see how they sterilized me, too? Mark my words, Henryk: they're only interested in obliteration."

"The Jewish people have been through worse," Henryk waves away Martin's theory. "Even you, Martin, are proof that we can survive. We must put our faith in God, Viktor. There's no other way."

"Yes, there is," Martin says. "Outright refusal. We fight."

"Fight with what?" Calel chimes in. "They'll slaughter us like those refugees outside Warsaw."

"So be it," Martin says. "Better to die fighting than to comply with their demands. Nothing good can come of this council of Jewish elders."

"Unlike you, Martin," Henryk suggests, "Viktor and I have no choice. Our names are on their list, not to mention my responsibility to the community—no, let me finish, Martin—I have a *responsibility* to my community, whatever you think that means. So does Viktor."

"But I'm not Jewish," Viktor begins.

"They asked for your name specifically," Henryk

interrupts. "They need German speakers, and if you refuse, they'll simply shoot you and choose someone else. We need council members we can trust. It's your duty, Viktor ..."

Viktor reflects before speaking. "And what if Martin is right? What if we're the ones they intend to corrupt? First, we need to understand why they want this council in the first place."

Henryk shakes his head. "There's no time, Viktor. I've been ordered to report to the council with three names. They'll arrest my family if I don't show up. You have to come with me. They expect me to introduce you to the council president. They know where you live, Viktor. They'll come for you in any case."

Viktor is confused. "If the council hasn't been elected yet, how is there already a council president?"

Henryk fidgets in his seat and looks down at the table. "If you decide afterward that you don't want to—"

"That's a good question, Viktor," Martin says. "Tell us, Henryk. Who *is* the council president?"

Henryk sighs and stands to leave.

"Who is it?" Martin demands.

"It doesn't matter," Henryk sighs. "They've made their choice. Chaim Rumkowski, the former Helonowek orphanage director. All the more reason for you to help us, Viktor."

"You can't be serious," Martin laughs.

"Oh, don't tell me you believe those crazy rumors!" Henryk pleads.

"Oh, Henryk," Martin speaks to him like a child. "Do

you really believe that little girls can get gonorrhea from dirty linens?"

"He was acquitted!" Calel interjects.

The best Henryk can do is sigh. "Viktor, I know Rumkowski is an unpleasant man, but they've already made their choice. I'm asking you, Viktor, as a good, decent citizen—as a friend—to help. The council needs a German speaker and we have to protect this community. You don't have to believe in God to believe in the wisdom of Maimonides."

"Maimonides!" Martin howls. "What could he possibly say about putting the council in the hands of a child rapist?" Martin pushes his chair away from the table, takes a final swig of vodka, and points at Henryk. "You know what your problem is? You delude yourself into believing in the goodness of mankind when mankind just tried to slit your throat. And now you're trying to justify working for a pedophile hired by assassins. Your faith is nothing more than a delusion, and it'll be the death of you and the rest of your imagined *community*."

"Yes, perhaps," Henryk sneers. "But at least I'll die as part of a community. You're nothing more than a lonely faggot. I don't know why Viktor bothers with you, really!"

Martin smiles victoriously. "You hear that, Viktor? So *that's* what it's all about, is it? A question of morality? This council is a trap, Viktor. They're already turning us against each other."

"Enough now, the both of you," Viktor manages to stand on his feet. "Henryk, I'll do you this favor and meet with Rumkowski as a courtesy, but I agree with Martin: no good can come from joining a Nazi-imposed council."

Carl is sitting at the end of a long dining table in an abandoned school cafeteria with an unexploded artillery shell in the center of the room. Most of the bombs landed in the playground and blew in all of the windows, covering the floor with shards of glass. Carl's hulking, muscular body is much too large for the child-sized seating. Here, he feels like a giant in a miniature land. It's been hard finding time to write Elsa these past weeks, what with the long days of round-ups and constant relocating. The battalion commander has deemed personal letters security risks, but still, Carl keeps writing, at least for himself. He has to get everything down on paper before it's too late; wants to tell Elsa the simple truth: *darling, I'm afraid.*

He writes quickly as a group of soldiers approaches.

I am sorry for what happened at the hotel and at your office, Elsa. I didn't mean to get you in trouble with Major Brandt. The truth is, I'm afraid I'll never—

"Hey, Becker! Get out of here," an officer enters the cafeteria with his squad. "What exactly are you writing, anyway?"

Carl crumples up the letter and smashes it into his jacket pocket. "Nobody. Nothing, I mean."

The officer looks at Carl inquisitively and laughs. "At ease. I'm just messing with you, Becker. I've got someone back home, too."

The officer and his men gather around a large regional map at the end of the table. As Carl walks away, he looks over his shoulder to watch the commander point out various locations on the map. "You know the drill," the commander says. "We'll hit Zgiersk, Pabianice, Brzeziny, Piotrków

Trybunalski. Pacify the artists and intellectuals and anyone who tries to resist, but take the Jews to the headquarters in Radogoszcz, just north of Bałuty."

Carl lingers to listen at the cafeteria entrance.

"Why can't we just shoot them in the woods?"

"*Pacify*, Scholtz," the commander corrects him. "The word we use is *pacify*. Is that understood? Hey, Becker! Didn't I tell you to get out of here?"

Carl's booted footsteps echo through the abandoned corridors of the primary school. He passes empty class-rooms with unfinished alphabets and unsolved equations on the chalkboards. Though the sun is up, most of the men are still sleeping, taking advantage of a lazy morn-ing before heading back towards Łódź. The city is now called *Litzmannstadt* in honor of a dead German general, and thousands of eager Germans are already emigrating to the region in hopes of being placed in Hitler's "Jewel of the East." But first, the *Volksdeutsche* will be placed in tem-porary housing facilities in nearby Pabianice, whose train station connects *Litzmannstadt* to the rest of the *Reichsgau Wartheland*.

Carl sits down in a small classroom to finish Elsa's letter:

I'm afraid I'll never see you again. Darling, I miss you. I miss your warmth. Out here in the Polish countryside, it's a different kind of cold. It seeps into your bones and under your skin. It makes me miss home. Do you remember that day by the lake? I still think about it often. I see you everywhere out here, darling … in a reflection in a shop window, in the way the leaves fall off the trees, in the tracks left by a villager's footsteps in the mud. The days are long. The skies are gray. It can be so lonely out here, my darling. Cornelius and I have developed a strong friendship, but perhaps friendship isn't the right word. We look out for each other, though. Some of the men are so young. I still prefer to be alone most of the time. I have grown accustomed to the night. Something about it calms me. In the darkness, when there's nothing to see, it all starts to make sense, somehow. That's when I see us together again. If you agree to meet me again, my darling, I promise I can change. The security services confiscated my last letter to you. I am writing to tell you that I am different now. I can feel it. I am no longer drinking as much as I used to. You would be proud. How many weeks has it been since I last kissed you? Will you give me one more chance?

I love you,

C

He tucks the letter into his chest pocket and returns to the schoolyard, where troop transports have arrived to ferry the battalion to Pabianice. During the four-hour drive through frost-bitten hills and windblown forests, Carl gets car-sick playing cards with Cornelius and a young recruit who keeps asking about what's happening in the Lagiewnicki woods.

"You don't have enough hair on your chest to know the answer," Cornelius laughs.

"No more cards for me," Carl hiccups.

"Stop being a cunt," Cornelius punches Carl in the shoulder. "Take this. It helps." He hands Carl half of a grainy white pill.

"Is it for nausea?"

"Yes," Cornelius smiles.

Carl swallows the pill and soon feels much better. His mind clear and sharp, he loses himself in the passing countryside and more rounds of cards and canteens of vodka and vapid conversation.

As the effects of Cornelius' little white pill start to fade, Carl succumbs to a strange hollowness in the pit of his stomach.

"Can I have some water?" He asks, but Cornelius gives him vodka instead. His heart now racing, he focuses on his breathing, just like Elsa taught him, in through his nose and out through his mouth, over and over and over again.

"Everybody out!" The battalion commander welcomes them to the Pabianice train station. "Now listen up. Hundreds of thousands of *Volksdeutsche* will pass through this station in the next months. We are the faces of the New Germany, and we will be the first to welcome them with a smile! Our comrades have been on a long journey to reach the frontier, so make sure you answer their questions and keep your tally counters up to speed. Each of you is responsible for recording and filing your numbers at the end of the day."

Carl's heart is still racing. He lights a cigarette and takes another swig of vodka as the men crunch across the frozen ground towards the railway. The cold wind reminds him of Danzig, and of his mother, and of the fireplace in their childhood home, and of the way she used to hold him at the hearth and stroke his hair. Head throbbing, he floats in a stupor towards the approaching trains, remembering a time when the screech of a train whistle signaled adventure.

"Hey, Carl! Over here!" Cornelius waves at him through a cloud of steam and Carl can barely hear him over the white noise of the churning engines.

"I traded for more!" Cornelius waves a fresh tube of pills in Carl's face. "He didn't know we get booze for free. What an idiot!"

Carl waves away the pills. "The nausea is gone, but I still feel a bit strange ..."

"It's not a nausea pill, you idiot! It's a Stuka tablet. There's going to be *two thousand people* checking in today. Take a whole one and chew it."

"Will it make my headache go away?"

"Sure it will. Have some vodka to wash it down."

The crunch of the pill is metallic and awful and the effect almost immediate: a surge of energy from Carl's feet to his fingers, which finds power in his sternum and makes him feel weightless again, motivated even.

The hours pass quickly. Curious faces appear in the train windows as the locomotives arrive one by one, but Carl is surprised at just how poor and tired these ethnic Germans seem, at how few personal effects they've brought with them to the new German frontier. By the time he goes on break, his tally counter is well over four hundred; whenever Carl feels weak, he takes another fresh Stuka tablet to save him. The drug is a godsend for such tedious labor—it almost makes it interesting—but time plays tricks on him, at once speeding up and slowing down.

"Do you really believe these people are Aryans?" Cornelius asks after processing a particularly destitute group from Volhynia. "They look like *Untermenschen*, don't you think? Something's wrong with this batch."

Carl shrugs. "Can you really tell the difference between an eastern German and a western Pole just by looking at them?"

"Of course *I* can't, but that's why we have scientists. What I'm saying is, somebody isn't doing their job on the other end, sending such lousy specimens to the frontier."

Carl's headache is bubbling to the surface again. He chews his last remaining tablet and rubs the residue on his gums, tongues at the bitter paste caked between his molars. Carl pinches his nose and blows hard to try and alleviate the mounting pressure in his head as a high-pitched ringing explodes from somewhere inside his skull.

His vision blurs. He stumbles backward and swallows hard, but his throat's too dry—he needs water—and he can no longer separate the sounds inside his head from the cooling hiss of the steam engines.

Cornelius slaps Carl across the face. "Hey, snap out of it, you idiot. You nearly stumbled onto the tracks."

"I'm fine," Carl insists. "Do you have any more?"

Cornelius laughs. "Have some lightning water. It lasts longer if you drink it."

Carl takes a long swig of the liquid metal until the canteen is almost empty.

"Save some for me!" Cornelius snatches it back from him. "You're crazier than you look, Becker."

identity

~~"I want to be somebody like somebody else was once."~~

~~—Kaspar Hauser~~

"Perhaps all the dragons in our lives are princesses who are only waiting to see us act, just once, with beauty and courage. Perhaps everything that frightens us is, in its deepest essence, something helpless that wants our love."

—Rainer Maria Rilke, *Letters to a Young Poet*, 1929

~~On May 26, 1828, a teenage foundling appeared out of nowhere in the streets of Nuremberg. The boy could only speak a few words: "Horse! Horse!" he screamed. He said he wanted to be like his father, a cavalryman, but the boy's strange, hunched-over way of moving about the world led the authorities to call him a feral child, a halfwit, a freak. The boy carried with him two letters alleging that he'd been held captive for the first sixteen years of his life. He could only write with assistance, his hand held by someone else. He wrote his name as Kaspar Hauser, but unable to communicate his past or explain his own identity, Kaspar was imprisoned as a vagabond, and his history was written for him. He was compared to Romulus, a boy raised by wolves, and gained notoriety in Germany and beyond as a~~

~~circus act. As the years went by, Kaspar caught the atten-~~
~~tion of a renowned legal scholar, Johann Anselm Ritter von~~
~~Feuerbach, who took the boy under his wing, educated him,~~
~~and wrote the seminal text on Kaspar's life: *The Wild Child:*~~
~~*The Unsolved Mystery of Kaspar Hauser.* One year after its pub-~~
~~lication, Feuerbach died under mysterious circumstances.~~
~~A few months later, Kaspar also succumbed to an untimely~~
~~death. The life and death of Kaspar Hauser remains one of~~
~~the great mysteries of the nineteenth century. So, who was~~
~~Kaspar Hauser, *really*? And how can we know his truth if~~
~~he couldn't tell it?~~

I thought telling Kaspar Hauser's story might give me
permission to tell my own, but it only took me further away
from making sense of the beginning. In Greek mytholo-
gy, the mother of the Muses is Mnemosyne, memory, the
supreme being of inspiration. The ancients believed that
when we drink from the river of memory, we halt the trans-
migration of the soul. In other words, to remember is to
stop time, if only momentarily. But whenever I began to
recall that boy at the bookshelf, the teakettle would boil,
the phone would ring, the sirens would begin, and the past
was shelved once again.

As a master's student in London, I found myself face-
to-face with the question of what it meant to be me.
Somewhere along my academic journey studying modern
German history, I'd lost my childlike wonder of peering
into the unknown. Back home, my mother's health continued to decline, and even if she'd helped me remember how
Viktor and Elsa first came to me, what right did I have to
recount the history of the Łódź Ghetto (in a book of fiction, no less), and how dare I invent historical characters in
hopes of approximating personal truth? What was worse,

my esteemed professor harshly criticized my thesis that focused on a reserve police battalion and told me there was no use in getting a master's if I didn't plan on pursuing a Ph.D.

Dejected and disheartened, on a cold day in February, I walked up the concrete stairwell of my dormitory in Kentish Town and found an old mirror discarded on the fourth-floor landing. Surprised that someone would throw away such a beautiful antique—there were detailed vines and flowers carved into the ornate wooden frame—I knocked on the neighbor's door. A woman with a bath towel wrapped around her head greeted me. She said she was throwing away the mirror because of the cracked frame and the stripped red paint.

I knew I couldn't keep the mirror when I left London, but I took it anyway. Somehow, I felt connected to it, as if it had special powers, like Ovid's myth of Narcissus, wherein the reflection becomes a totem of obsession and vanity. Or maybe it was like the painting in *The Picture of Dorian Gray*, or perhaps a mystical portal to another realm, like in Lewis Carrol's *Through the Looking Glass*. Sitting in front of that mirror in my dreary dormitory, I thought of Bram Stoker's *Dracula*, in which only creatures with a soul can see their reflection, but I settled on my favorite interpretation, *Harry Potter's* Mirror of Erised, which shows the seeker what they truly desire.

During those last weeks in London, I found solace sitting in front of that mirror, remembering how my first love was fiction, not history. I returned to old classics like Mary Shelley and Franz Kafka and modern masters like Salman Rushdie and Julian Barnes; and then, on one gray morning of no particular importance, the first sentence of this book finally came to me: When the sirens began, the professor was sitting at the Astoria Café.

Viktor is dressed in black for a funeral he doesn't know he's attending. His black leather shoes are already caked in frosty mud and his toes grow colder as he roams through the narrow streets of Bałuty. Whenever he passes a German patrol on the boulevard, he steps off the sidewalk and into the slushy gutter to salute his oppressors. They look him over with a disgusted kind of curiosity, waiting for him to make a mistake. Bałuty has been chosen as the site for the new ghetto, and Viktor has been deemed Jewish by the Nazi authorities on account of two grandparents he never knew. It no longer matters what Viktor thinks about his identity—in the eyes of the law, Viktor is now an *Untermensch* required to wear a white armband with a Star of David at all times. Just two days ago, two men were attacked for concealing their armbands in an "Aryans-only" shop. Yesterday, Viktor saw them hanging by a lamp post. Today, their frozen corpses creak in the wind.

Since last month's attack at the Astoria, Viktor has been staying inside as much as possible. Henryk disappeared for two weeks before reappearing with fresh scars and an unshakable conviction to join the Nazi-imposed ghetto council. Since then, fourteen of Viktor's colleagues (all of them Gentiles) have disappeared, and Viktor is the only professor he knows who hasn't been arrested or gone into hiding (his neighbor, Mrs. Eberhardt, hasn't made so much as a peep since their last encounter). Still, Viktor fears it's only a matter of time, which is why he's headed to Tadeusz and Rachel's on the tree-lined boulevard of ~~Piotrkowska~~

~~Street~~ *Adolf-Hitler-Straße* to discuss their escape out of the city. Before entering the elegant lobby with high ceilings, Viktor removes his cold, soiled shoes and wrings out his black socks at the entrance.

There's no doorman today. Viktor walks across the red-carpeted lobby with dripping shoes in hand and is visited by an unwanted memory. Even before the building was occupied, Viktor avoided coming here; just the rumbling of the elevator's metallic cage is enough to transport him back to that last morning with Helen.

Both of their hearts were broken then and there at the station, back when Helen trusted him most. The day was cold and the London skies were heavy with rain. He said he was taking her to the countryside for the weekend, but this was a lie. So was the pill he gave her for motion sickness on the train. Thanks to the sedative, Helen didn't realize their destination wasn't a hotel until after the caged elevator closed shut.

Viktor shudders at the sound of the infernal lift as it rattles towards Rachel and Tadeusz's floor. He used to think of himself as a noble psychiatrist, but he stopped being a true doctor the day he betrayed Helen. If he'd been a respectable medical practitioner, if he'd upheld his oath to care for and protect, he never would have brought her there, never would have put her in that cage and pleaded with her to remain calm as she thrashed and screamed.

"She's going to be fine," the head surgeon reassured him. "You've done everything you can, Dr. Bauman. She's in good hands. There's a clinic we are working with in Portugal. She'll be treated there. And not to worry: we're only concerned with the prefrontal lobe."

What terrifies Viktor most to this day is, in that moment, he actually believed them.

But what else could he have done? He'd already tried insulin injections in Paris and a combination of malarial therapy and barbiturates in Brussels. After that, he placed his faith in the science of an icepick and a scooper.

Barbarity in the name of love.

A fate worse than death. And how spectral she looked when he visited her on that rocky coastline, standing pale like a ghost with her crooked smile and childlike confusion. The esteemed lobotomist appeared by her side and told her to wave goodbye to Viktor. A week later, Viktor resigned from his psychiatry position at Kings College and took a job teaching history in Poland.

That was five years ago. The lift jolts to a halt and only now does Viktor realize there's no lift attendant either. Viktor is cautious as he tiptoes to Rachel and Tadeusz's apartment down the hallway. The door is ajar and his eyes are drawn to the shimmer of broken glass in the carpet at the entryway. Viktor picks up a shattered picture frame: a portrait of Rachel, tall and thin, holding Little Tadeusz's and Ania's hands, both looking up at her in reverence.

"Rachel? Tadeusz?" He calls out and approaches the kitchen at the end of the hall. Some of the cabinets have been ripped out entirely. *Did they escape?*

In the spacious carpeted dining room, Viktor inspects a long gash along the wall as if someone had circled the entire room dragging a blade. Something sharp had been used to hack at the dining table, too, scattering small chunks of wood and splinters all over the floor.

In the adjacent room, it's more of the same: a

disemboweled sofa and an upended bookcase that crushed a pot of flowers, caking mounds of dirt into the room's cream-colored rug. Viktor continues into the bedroom, sits on the edge of the double bed, picks up a clump of feathers from the shredded mattress, and rubs the soft mass between his fingers.

"Rachel, Tadeusz?"

A faint voice emerges from somewhere within Tadeusz's elegant, hand-carved wardrobe. "We're here, Viktor."

Viktor steps into the wardrobe and pushes past thick winter coats.

"To the left on the back wall, there's a small hole," Tadeusz's muffled voice calls out.

Viktor runs his palms along the back wooden panel and feels for a small carved hole in the musty darkness.

"I want out!" Little Ania begins crying.

"I'm coming, my little one. Tadeusz, how do I open it?"

"There's a small hole at waist height, about the size of your index finger."

Viktor stops trying to search with his palms and instead drags the tips of his fingers along the wood until his pointer finger finds the indentation of a small carved hole. With some effort, Viktor manages to wrench open the secret sliding panel. Tadeusz tumbles out first, and then Rachel, and then the children, all of them gasping for air.

"Uncle Viktor!" Little Tadeusz jumps into his arms. Little Ania whoops and giggles and bounces around the bedroom, picking up clumps of the bedding's feathers, tossing them above her head and dancing beneath the floating wisps.

"You saved us," Rachel hugs Viktor. "We were starting to suffocate. Six hours we've been huddling in there, thanks to Tadeusz's *ingenious* invention."

"We're alive, aren't we?" Tadeusz is offended. "I told you the door isn't finished yet."

"Was it the Gestapo?" Viktor asks.

"Looters," Tadeusz says.

"Not in front of the children," Rachel whispers. "Okay, little ones. Stay in the bedroom with your father and clean up these feathers. Uncle Viktor and I need to talk."

"I'm going to get all the feathers!" Ania yelps. "I'm going to be the Feather Princess!"

Little Tadeusz jumps up and down in excitement, too. "And *I'm* going to be the prince!" He grabs Ania's hands and spins her around in circles. Viktor relishes in the innocent moment before following Rachel into the kitchen.

"He won't listen to me, Viktor," Rachel's voice shakes. "I've been telling him for weeks we have to get out of the city. The French aren't coming and—take that thing off your arm, Viktor! Are you crazy?"

Rachel rips off Viktor's Star of David armband and shoves it into his jacket pocket.

"The looters will attack you if they see it," Rachel says. "A gang of them have been threatening us for weeks. They finally came last night. Kicked down the door at four in the morning. Every Jewish home in the neighborhood is being ransacked. Tadeusz doesn't get it. We have to leave *now*."

Rachel collapses into a chair at the kitchen table as Tadeusz arrives.

"I know, Rachel. I'm sorry. We'll go to Sasha's cellar at

the bakery. I just spoke with him on the telephone. Professor Borowski is there, too."

"There's not enough space for all of us. We have to get out of the city *tonight*."

"And go where?" Tadeusz sits across from her at the small, circular table. "They're hunting Jews in the country-side and sending them back into the city."

"He's right," Viktor says. "Until now, they've been focusing on the academic community, but Jewish families will surely be next. Rumors are they're building a ghetto. Most of the senior faculty is dead. Hundreds of artists and intellectuals have disappeared, too. I think it's still safer here in the city."

"Look at the street names," Rachel shakes her head. "We can't stay here."

"But why send German migrants into the city?" Tadeusz wonders. "If they're building a ghetto ... it doesn't make any sense."

"It's not supposed to make sense. They're sowing confusion. They want us to submit."

"That's why we have to be smart," Tadeusz replies. "For at least tonight, we'll go to Sasha's cellar."

"You're impossible, Tadeusz," Rachel scoffs. "Talk some sense into him, Viktor. The Gestapo probably already knows about the bakery. Tell him, Viktor."

But Viktor doesn't know. As Rachel waits for him to say something wise or take her side, he remains silent, uncomfortable consoling others because he doesn't know how to console himself.

"You always take his side," Rachel storms out of the kitchen.

"What's the name of the town where your mother lives?" Viktor asks Tadeusz.

"Wymagamówka. But it's out of the question, Viktor. Even if, by some miracle, my psychotic mother doesn't rat us out immediately, her dementia is an utter liability. Not to mention the neighbors."

"You said the caretaker was a decent man, right? Is he still there? Rachel does have a point, Tadeusz. Sasha's cellar might not be safe, what with the Rubins and the Borowskis already there."

Tadeusz goes to the cabinet below the sink and pulls out a bottle of vodka. "The bastards didn't look that hard. I haven't spoken to the caretaker in years." He returns to the table with three glasses. "The last time I saw my mother was just before the wedding. That was eight years ago, Viktor. She called me a Jew-loving Bolshevik. She renounced me—her only son. You have no idea what kind of woman we're dealing with."

"Yes, but the caretaker can safely hide you. Rachel isn't wrong: this is only going to get worse. *Lebensraum*, Tadeusz. Just do me a favor and call the caretaker."

Tadeusz agrees, begrudgingly. The sound of dialing the phone's rotary reminds Viktor of Helen again. *Not now. Not here.* Helen had trashed the apartment and locked herself in the bathroom with a knife. He had to call the police. Viktor shakes the memory from his mind and digs his bare toes into the kitchen floor. He focuses on being present, on listening to Tadeusz's conversation.

"Yes, we are safe. Is Mother dead yet? We don't know what else to do."

Before Tadeusz hangs up, Rachel appears at the kitchen

threshold with terror in her eyes—the sound of heavy trucks coming to a halt outside, doors opening and closing, harsh German voices and barking dogs.

"Rachel," Tadeusz grabs her by the shoulders. "Take the children to the wardrobe. We'll stall them."

"No," Viktor says. "Put on warm clothes and take them to the roof. I'll stall them, Tadeusz. We're not debating this."

Viktor crouches to speak to Little Tadeusz and Ania. "We're going to play a different game now, okay? It's called the princess and the dragon." Viktor strokes Little Tadeusz's forehead. "Don't be scared. It's a game. Are you ready for the rules? The castle is this building, and your mother is the princess. We have to protect her from the dragons. Are you ready?"

"Yes."

"When you get to the top of the castle, on the roof, it's very important not to make any noise."

Rachel holds back tears.

"Not even a whisper," Viktor says. "Can you promise me that?"

"Yes."

"Can you both show me how good you are at being quiet?"

"Yes."

Little Tadeusz inhales deeply, puffs out his cheeks, and suppresses a giggle. The sound of screaming voices reverberates from below.

"Rachel, we have to go," Tadeusz grabs her.

"Go now," Viktor hugs them. "You'll see from the roof

if they take me. Whatever you do, don't come out until they've left. Understand? Go!"

Viktor runs with the family to the front door and watches them disappear at the end of the corridor. Only once he's back in the kitchen does he realize he's cut his feet. He pours himself a shot of vodka and winces in pain as he removes the biggest piece of glass from his heel. Viktor pours another shot and raises his glass to the empty room as violent banging arrives at the front door.

Viktor throws back the shot, swallows hard, and approaches his fate.

Adrenaline courses through him. A past life in each step. He searches for a happy memory: he was just a boy standing at the top of a carpeted stairwell. It was his birthday. He dug his toes into the carpet, and on that carpet, he tried to run while playing tag, tripped, and crushed his big toe beneath his foot, snapping the ligament. On that very carpet—*or this one, was it not?*—he first learned how to walk, back when the world felt like a sandbox, a place to play, and though his eyes are closed, and though the world outside is shaking, it was also here, on this very carpet, *was it not?* that he made love to Helen in a hotel room in Paris. He savors the memory of how her lush hair seemed to melt into the floor, and Viktor is calm when he opens the door.

He greets the two Gestapo officers with a smile, one of whom is clean-shaven and good-looking, the other bald and red-faced. The handsome one looks like a movie star, his lapel covered in patches, pins, and medals.

"*Guten tag*, officers. How can I be of service?" Viktor says in perfect German.

"Your name," the commanding officer demands.

"Viktor Bauman."

"Is that so?" The chubby, red-faced officer looks him over suspiciously. "That name isn't on the registry. Are you a Jew? Where's your armband? Why are you here? How do you speak German so well?"

"I was born in Austria."

"An Austrian Jew, is it?"

"I never said I was Jewish."

"Whatever you are, Austrian, you're coming with us," the commander grabs Viktor by the forearm.

"May I put on some shoes?"

"No need for that. Lieutenant, check the apartment and then the roof. The family living in this apartment remains unaccounted for …"

Viktor's eyes dart wildly in search of something to delay them. "Officers," he says, pointing to the window at the end of the hall. "The only roof access is over there, by the fire escape. But I'd be careful. The rungs are weak and frozen … it's quite dangerous."

The commanding officer tightens his grip on Viktor's forearm. "The Austrian is lying. Surely we can access the rooftop from the stairwell." He twists Viktor's arm behind his back. "Someone you know hiding up there, perhaps?"

Viktor moans as he's led down the stairs, his twisted forearm tendons threatening to snap. With each step, the shards of glass press further into his foot, and whatever lofty delusions of meaning Viktor had walking along that carpet have disappeared. Now, he feels like an animal with a singular purpose: stop the pain coursing through his body. Survive.

They stop at the landing below, where the pianist Joel Bronstein is leaning on the door frame with a handkerchief pressed to his bloody forehead.

"He's lucky," the officer tells Viktor. "Normally, I would've shot him on the spot, but I thought I could use you both first. You have one hour to vacate this apartment. You are not to use the elevator, and if you break or steal any valuables, you will be shot. Is that understood?"

The officer marches down the stairs.

"Have some water, Viktor," Joel leads him into his lavish apartment. "I already packed most of the boxes weeks ago. We'll throw the clothing directly out of the window. We just have to get a few cabinets out, and then the desk. They're keeping the piano and the porcelain and the armoire and the bed … apparently, the most valuable objects in a Jewish home aren't infected."

Viktor and Joel work at a superhuman pace. Joel is much older than Viktor and struggles to catch his breath going up and down the four flights of stairs, but Viktor bears the brunt of the weight. "Joel, you can bear this," he reassures the pianist after dumping two leather chairs into the snow. Each time Viktor ascends the stairwell, he prays for silence. So long as his footsteps reverberate to the top floor, there's hope that Rachel, Tadeusz, and the children have managed to stay hidden.

Miraculously, by the end of the hour, Joel's apartment is empty. Outside in the snow, Joel crumples to the ground.

Viktor lifts Joel by the armpits and sits him in a chair. He looks down at his feet, purple and numb, and steps onto the pile of clothing tossed from the window to warm them, rocking from one foot to the other to increase circulation, glancing up at the rooftop for any sign of Rachel or Tadeusz. No luck.

"Who told you to sit!" The commander sprints from the building entrance and shoves his pistol into Joel's temple. "Stand straight. And you, Austrian, I know what you're doing. Get off that pile of clothing." The commander glances at his wristwatch. "By my count, you still have four minutes before the hour is up. So let's play a game: each of you, pick up one of those wooden chairs and hold them straight out in front of your face. I'll give you three minutes. If you don't drop the chair, I solemnly swear I won't shoot you in the head."

Joel's forearms shake as he raises the wooden chair into the air. Viktor opens his mouth to tell Joel that he can bear this, but the exhaustion is setting in, and he can only groan.

The first minute goes quickly, until the commanding officer's portly, red-faced minion exits the building with Tadeusz and hurls him face-first into the snow.

"He tried to fight me!" He tells his commander. "I found him hiding on the roof! He was trying to cover his tracks."

The commander smiles, lights a cigarette, and cocks his pistol. "Get him on his knees. He can play, too. If any of you make so much as a sound for the next two minutes, I start shooting. Is that a deal?" The commander looks at his watch. "Annnnd, go!"

Viktor grits his teeth and digs his swollen toes into the snow. He doesn't have any memory to cling to, just the swirling cigarette smoke the officer is blowing into his face. *Viktor, you can bear this.*

The officer moves on to Joel, who utters a feeble moan

as the officer presses the burning cigarette to his forehead.

"Did you hear that? No? I swear I heard something," the commander re-applies the burning cigarette to Joel's cheek, but Joel remains silent. His effort is heroic.

"I'm impressed," the commander says. "You people are stronger than I thought. Eighty-three seconds left. Eight-two. Eighty-one. Do you think you can hold on, pianist? How about a final test?"

The commander walks over to the pile of Joel's belongings, picks up a stack of books, and places it atop Joel's trembling chair.

Joel's knees wobble and buckle. He lets out a terrible groan.

"He made a sound!" The commander's minion yelps with glee and kicks Tadeusz in the mouth. "Did you hear that, sir? He made a sound!"

Viktor focuses on the time he has left. *Fifty-nine. Fifty-eight. Fifty-seven—*

"This one looks cold," the fat officer loosens his belt and begins pissing on Tadeusz.

Thirty-four. Thirty-three.

Tadeusz remains silent beneath the stream of urine. Joel's stack of books finally thuds to the snow.

"Ah, what a shame …" the commander says. "And only twenty seconds to go. Well, rules are rules."

"Shoot me, you coward," Tadeusz sputters.

"Very well then," the commander turns to Tadeusz with a vicious smile and cocks his pistol.

"Viktor, listen to me," Tadeusz is calm. "When you see my mother, tell her I said hello."

Viktor has trouble computing what he sees next. He hasn't seen death before, not up close, only read about it in books and dreamt of it in nightmares. The first thought Viktor has when the gunshot rings out and Tadeusz's body slumps to the ground is: *there wasn't any blood.* Tadeusz's eyes are still open and his body is still twitching and there's no blood to speak of—*this can't be real.*

The only evidence of Tadeusz's murder is a bloodless, coin-sized hole burrowed into his forehead. The commander turns to Joel and takes aim.

"Don't let them have my piano, Viktor," Joel pleads.

The gunshot goes off right next to Viktor's ear.

Joel falls like a whisper into the snow.

"Austrian," the commander slaps Viktor in the face. "Your time is up. You can let go of the chair now. I told you I'd keep my promise."

Viktor drops the chair and collapses to the ground in exhaustion.

"We know who you are, Bauman. You are expected at the *Judenrat* tomorrow. Your colleague, Henryk Dawidowicz, has arranged a meeting with the president. If you fail to appear, I'll personally hang both of you by a lamppost."

The commander spits on Viktor and turns to his underling. "Get some petrol from the car and burn clothing and furniture. Throw in the bodies, too."

Viktor is delirious with shock. He feels nothing. The first thought he has when Joel and Tadeusz are thrown onto the blazing pyre is that perhaps they'll be warmed by the flames. He remains curled up in the snow for a long time— twenty minutes? forty minutes? he cannot know—until the sound of gunfire echoing through the empty streets brings him back to the fore. The raging pyre fills Viktor with momentary clarity and conviction. Before stumbling home, he returns to Joel's apartment to honor the pianist's dying wish.

The winter months have begun to muffle something in Carl's spirit. The sun rises far too late and sets far too early; only an eternal gray sky colors his walks to the Pabianice train station. Carl doesn't bother looking up for patches of blue anymore because he knows they aren't there, and time keeps playing tricks on him, slowing down when he believes the day is almost over, speeding up when he's safe and warm in his bed. In one moment, he's escorting migrants along the train platform, and in the next, he's walking a nameless *Volksdeutsch* back to a dingy hotel room; then it's morning again, and his bed sheets are soaked with sweat, and his pillow smells like sweet poison, and with each successive young woman Carl fucks, he erases yet another memory of Elsa.

He wants to make amends and begin again, but he doesn't know how. Elsa refuses to see him, and the last time he tried to speak to her, she threatened to involve the SS. In a sober moment of clarity after a particularly harrowing night with a young migrant from Munich, Carl jots down a few sentences he doesn't dare admit to his sober self: *I don't recognize myself anymore. The others look at me differently, too. I've been away from home for too long. This is not the way I envisioned it. It was supposed to be different. The world is slipping away from me. Perhaps I am too.*

Carl replaces his coffee with a Stuka tablet, which

he now knows is Pervitin, an amphetamine. He arrives at Pabianice just as a train is pulling up to the platform and barely registers the sound of the train whistle. The steam envelops him. According to the manifest, today's migrants are coming from a region called Galicia. Carl has never heard of it, and he agrees with Cornelius that these *Volksdeutsche* don't look like the pure-bloods from Germany. He interrogates one family that seems particularly suspect and punches a teenage boy in the face who talks back at him (when the boy's sister tries to protect her brother, Carl thrusts her up against the wall and threatens to teach her a lesson her body won't forget).

He hates these travelers and has grown callous and tired of all these young people questioning his authority. On his break, Carl relieves himself behind the station and stares at the shriveled state of his manhood, the sight of which sobers him enough to feel ashamed of his behavior, if only momentarily. *I know I can be better.* He wants to believe it. But he also knows that yesterday, he grabbed the young woman too roughly in the showers, and he knows he shouldn't have put his mouth on her, either—she was too young—but he didn't really *do anything*, did he? all he did was try to kiss her—maybe he groped her momentarily—and yes, he admitted to his commanding officer that he shouldn't have pressed himself up against her naked body in the showers, but he won't berate himself for it, not in the land of the *Untermenschen*, because lots of other men do it, —officers, even—and Carl is a policeman who demands respect.

Carl smashes his limp cock back through the cold buttons of his fly, takes a swig from his flask, and makes his way to the soccer stadium for another day of registrations.

For the past weeks (how many exactly he can't remember), Carl and Cornelius have been sitting at fold-out tables on a soccer pitch, registering migrant names by the thousands, ten hours a day. In December alone, Carl recorded over three thousand *Volksdeutsche*. Today, however, he and Cornelius are on security detail, which means all he has to do is stand with a rifle atop the stadium. The buzz of confusion fades away as they hike to the top, careful not to slip on the icy, concrete steps.

"Sausage? Have some. It's about to go bad," Cornelius waves a moldy, pink bratwurst in Carl's face.

"No thanks."

"Suit yourself," Cornelius rips into the sausage with his back molars and chews with his mouth open; the smell reminds Carl of the latrines. Carl lights a cigarette and re-ups on the Pervitin, which first takes effect in Carl's fingertips, then his belly, and up into his head. Paired with the nicotine, alcohol, Carl finds purpose in peering down at the eddy of human beings swirling about the soccer pitch; he has a vision of himself and Cornelius mowing them down with machine guns. *If they weren't here, we could go home. And who are these people, anyway, these strangers in my city? And why do they keep asking so many questions?* Like a hawk surveying its prey, Carl takes aim with his rifle and pretends to shoot those leaving the stadium in the back of the head.

"You ever killed anyone?" Cornelius asks.

"No," Carl shakes his head and snatches the last bite of sausage from Cornelius' hand (he knows better than to ask Cornelius the same question). The cold meat is hard to chew, and the fat gets stuck in his teeth. Carl's jaw has been locking all week. After swallowing, he squats and swings his arms to keep himself warm, his flailing limbs silhou-etted against the backdrop of the winter sky. A pinprick of sunlight sneaks out from the grayness above, and with his blood pumping and the Pervitin coursing through his veins, Carl feels something resembling happiness. *Spring is coming. I can feel it. I'm coming back to you, Elsa. Remember that first night we met at the prison? I took your hand during the interrogation.*

Carl closes his eyes and imagines holding her in his arms. His pants grow tight, and when Cornelius isn't look-ing, Carl slides his hand into his front pocket to feel his growing erection. He takes a deep breath and imagines what he must look like, standing there atop the stadium like a king, his face masked by plumes of smoke and the cold vapor of his breath, his muscular chest puffed outwards, his throbbing erection lording over the human ants down below.

On the walk down the frozen steps, he doesn't even consider the possibility of slipping as he stalks a group of female migrants towards the shower facilities.

"How lucky are *we*?" Cornelius punches Carl in the shoulder as they gawk like pubescent boys at the naked bodies in the hot steam. At times, the women's bodies are entirely consumed by the vapor before it dissipates to reveal smooth skin and wet buttocks and swinging breasts. Carl's mind is laser-focused—he's seen a woman he particularly fancies—and in his hunger, he bets Cornelius a Pervitin tablet that he'll fuck her before nightfall.

"Did you see her over there," Cornelius points. "The blond. Third from the left. Just there, next to the fat one with long black hair. She's mine."

Carl squints through the stream, but his vision is blurry,

and his face is growing hot and his stomach lurches. The rank, undigested sausage is a stone in his belly. Carl loosens his neck collar to try and combat the heat as an all-too-familiar nausea overwhelms him. He stumbles along the wall of the showers, shoving past wet bodies and slippery skin, but at this moment he can only think of getting to the latrines.

Carl exits the showers and stumbles into the next room, a massive delousing chamber where migrants' clothing, luggage, and linens are sprayed with disinfectant. Amidst the hissing and tumbling roar of the laundry machines, Carl forgets about the invisible, noxious gases shimmering at the room's edges and vomits on himself before he can make it to the exit.

After relieving himself, he splashes cold water on his face. Staring down at his trembling hands and the amphetamines coursing through his veins, Carl clings to the sink for balance, sweating and shivering as the ground beneath him sways like a rowboat on a lake—*keep it together, Carl. Just take a deep breath.* Unmoored, Carl returns to the toilet to expel the rest of the rotten sausage. The smell makes him gag, but there's no vomit, only wretch.

Carl comes to in a chair in the temporary migrant housing facility, where Cornelius is handing him a cup of water and a piece of bread.

"You didn't eat enough again," Cornelius pats Carl on the shoulder. "I have just the solution. Look over there," Cornelius motions to the blond girl from the showers, who walks over tentatively.

"Don't be scared," Cornelius speaks to her as if she

were a child. "Where are you from, sweetheart? You must've come from far away. This is my friend, Carl. He needs somebody to take care of him."

Carl can barely see the face of the young woman standing in front of him.

"Hello, sir. I'm from Galicia," she says with a curtsy. "I'm from a small town on the River Bug."

"The River Bug! Well, isn't that nice?" Cornelius punches Carl in the arm. "Welcome to the New Reich, Young Beauty from the River Bug. My friend here couldn't help but notice you in the showers earlier." Cornelius chuckles. "Wouldn't you like to have a drink with him in the city?"

"No," Carl says. He doesn't have the energy to say anything more.

The teenager blushes and looks down at her feet.

"How was the train ride, sweetheart? Don't be shy," Cornelius insists.

"It was very pleasant, officer. Thank you."

"Oh yes?"

"Yes. After such a long train ride, the shower did me a world of good. I finally feel like a human being again."

"Yes, *a human being*," Cornelius squeezes the girl's face with his swollen hands. "Isn't that nice, Carl? Well, if there's anything you need—anything at all—you ask for Lieutenant Cornelius Landau, okay?"

Carl's vision swims as she walks away.

"Eat," Cornelius says.

Carl's jaw locks multiple times as he gnaws his way through the loaf. *Remember our first picnic by the lake together? I miss you, Elsa. I can be better.*

"You need to rest," Cornelius says. "The SS is inspecting the battalion tomorrow morning. It's time to see who's fit for the upcoming resettlement in Posen."

"Posen? No. We're supposed to be stationed in *Litzmannstadt*. I have to be there." *I'm coming, Elsa.* "Why are they sending us to Posen? I thought we were finished resettling the migrants."

"It's not that kind of resettlement, you idiot."

Elsa rushes to the hotel bathroom to vomit red wine. Last night, Major Brandt informed her she's being moved to a "more appropriate" location in the city, further from the nearly finished ghetto, effective immediately.

An early-morning phone call confirms her departure: a chauffeur will arrive in twenty minutes to bring her to her new apartment on *Adolf-Hitler-Straße*. After expelling all the poison from her stomach and taking a hot shower, Elsa has the concierge bring her hot tea. Instead of taking it on the sofa in the salon, like she usually does, Elsa puts the teacup on the bedside table, crawls back into bed, pulls the covers up to her neck, and puts a pillow over her head so that just for an instant, in this muffled darkness, she can imagine a different scenario, one in which she's elsewhere, far away from here.

It almost works. During her second sleep, she dreams of a sleigh ride with an old man in the Harz Forest—*is this the future?*—before being woken up by a loud banging at the door. The chauffeur waits in the hallway as Elsa dresses and throws her clothing into two large leather trunks.

During the short drive to her newly requisitioned

apartment, Elsa looks out the window at the boulevard's trees and their frail black limbs. Upon arrival, the chauffeur warns Elsa of the smoldering pile of debris and furniture next to the building. "Don't look. It's not pleasant," the chauffeur tries to direct her attention elsewhere, but Elsa has already spotted the two burnt corpses atop the pyre, their grimaced faces and charred limbs still glowing among the embers.

Inside the building, the chauffeur escorts Elsa into a caged elevator and up to her new apartment on the fourth floor. Its walls are barren save a few rectangular spots where works of art used to be. Cream-colored dropcloths have been laid out in preparation for wallpapering, including one draped over a grand piano at the room's center.

The chauffeur explains. "Furniture from the Municipal Bureau of Lodgings and Real Estate will be delivered once the painters are done. Do you play piano? It's a shame what they did to this one—who would destroy such a beautiful thing? We'll have it replaced if you so desire. As for now, I have to get you to Major Brandt."

"I think I'll walk. I feel a bit nauseous."

"I was told to drive you."

"I said I'll walk. Thank you."

The cold air does little to cure Elsa's hangover or quell her upset stomach as she passes the burnt corpses. Though the official construction of the ghetto isn't scheduled to begin for another week, thousands of people are already being crammed into the market district of Bałuty. Just around the corner from the Gestapo office on Zgierska, Elsa passes a man and a woman hanging from lampposts, their purple tongues lolling in their mouths, their faces taut like worn leather. She dry heaves at the rank smell of death and takes a moment to steel herself for yet another day with Major Brandt, with whom she can no longer pretend not to be complicit. Fragmented words of mass atrocities are becoming complete sentences, and despite the heavy drinking (two bottles per night), Elsa cannot reconcile her role in this nightmare, especially now that she's forced to sleep in a murdered man's home.

She can only try to resist as best she can. For the past few weeks, anytime someone comes into the office to denounce a neighbor, Elsa purposefully misspells names, misquotes addresses, and recombines information so that by the time the Gestapo receives the intelligence it's impossible to make sense of it. It's not much, but it might give Jewish families an extra couple of days to find a way out of the city before it's too late.

Perhaps more substantially, Elsa has found a way to hamper Brandt's fanaticism by doctoring his coffee with pills from his medicine cabinet. When she arrives at the office, in the privacy of the small office kitchen, Elsa grinds up the pills and dips her finger into the amphetamine powder to combat her hangover before using the rest to doctor Brandt's coffee.

"Miss Dietrich," the building's main receptionist, Frau Wolfmann, peeks inside the kitchen. "There's another *Volksdeutsch* outside with a complaint."

"Let them through." Elsa dabs another finger into the Pervitin and rubs it on her gums before greeting the old woman in a dusty black overcoat standing at her desk.

"Please, sit," Elsa says. Her mouth tastes of metal.

"Good morning, miss," the old woman takes a seat.

Her bone structure reminds Elsa of a bird of prey.

"What can I do for you?"

"My name is Hilda Eberhardt. I live with my husband. He is a war hero, in fact, a member of the same unit in 1915 that managed to—"

"I neither care about nor have time for inane details about your husband. What is it that you want?"

Mrs. Eberhardt purses her lips. "Very well. I have important information regarding a dangerous half-breed living in Bałuty."

"And do you live in Bałuty?" Elsa pretends to jot down the information.

"Well, no, not anymore."

"What is your address?"

"I live at 187 *Adolf-Hitler-Straße*. But I used to live on Pepper Street in Bałuty, where a half-breed stole from me and called me names. He's a Bolshevik academic, too. Surely you will find this useful information."

"As I am sure you are aware, Mrs. Eberhardt, there are much larger security issues at play than *personal grievances*. The Gestapo cannot consider every personal slight in this city."

"But the Jew stole from me!"

"So, it's a Jew, not a half-breed now?"

"Yes, but you don't understand. This half-breed is a Bolshevik! I saw his books. He must be punished. He speaks fluent German and entertains communists in his home."

"And what did you say his name was?"

"Bauman. Viktor Bauman. He is a former professor."

Elsa can't hide the smile hearing his name conjures.

"Ah, but of course!" Mrs. Eberhardt nods her head. "How foolish of me. The Gestapo must already be aware of Bauman. Perhaps there is an ongoing investigation? I knew I was right to come in."

Elsa stands up and comes around the desk to put her hand on Mrs. Eberhardt's spindly frame. "I can assure you, Mrs. Eberhardt, that we are aware of the situation and that I will personally see to it. This Bauman character will be found. He lives on Pepper Street, is it?"

"Yes, number sixteen. He lives on the top floor." The wrinkles in Mrs. Eberhardt's face soften. "And may I just say, what a relief it is to have *real* Germans working here in the land of the *Untermenschen*. And what is your name, Miss …?"

"Dietrich."

"Dietrich. A fine German name that is. Thank you, Miss Dietrich. And *Heil Hitler.*"

Elsa glances towards Brandt's office door, but there's no light coming from within. She doesn't salute.

"Thank you again for this information. I will personally tend to this matter immediately."

civilization

"First came news that the Jews believe—don't believe. After all, it is difficult to believe it; one has to see it with one's own eyes in order to have a clear idea how such things are possible and that, in the twentieth century."

—Calel Perechodnik, *Am I A Murderer?*: *Testament of a Jewish Ghetto Policeman*, 1942

The year is 2024 and the world is unraveling again. If we've learned anything as a species, it's how quickly we forget. Elvis Presley said animals don't hate and that we're supposed to be better than them, but if this were true, the history of fascist regimes wouldn't be so closely linked to the history of democratic elections.

In 1928, the Nazi Party won 2.6% of the parliamentary vote. In 1930, the number increased to 18%. In July 1932, the Nazi Party won 37% of the popular vote, securing 230 seats in the German Parliament, the *Reichstag*. When Hitler asked President Paul von Hindenburg to declare him chancellor, Hindenburg refused. Six months later, in January 1933, Hindenburg finally conceded to Hitler's demands just two months before a fresh round of parliamentary elections. The Nazis had already lost parliamentary seats in November 1932 and were at risk of losing more in the March 1933 elections. Six days before a democratic Germany went to the polls, a mysterious fire broke out in the *Reichstag.*

Hitler called it arson. Historians believe it was a false flag operation. Regardless, Hitler used the fire to convince Hindenburg to declare a state of emergency. The subsequent Reichstag Fire Decree was a pivotal entry in the fascist playbook: where there isn't clear and present danger, invent it. The Reichstag Fire Decree suspended all civil liberties, including freedom of expression, freedom of the press, the right to assembly, and the right to privacy in any postal, telegraphic, or telephonic communications. Now with a legal basis to conduct warrantless raids, Hitler could imprison loosely defined "criminals" and enforce the death penalty with impunity and could also overrule the German constitution itself if he deemed it in the country's "best interests."

The rise of the Third Reich's police state was swift and efficient. The *Reichstag* caught fire on Monday, February 27, 1933. By the end of the week, the first concentration camp was opened in the village of Nohra, Thuringia, and Dachau was opened a few weeks later. By the time Allied troops began liberating the first of some 40,000 concentration camps in 1944, the Nazis had systematically murdered over eleven million human beings.

The story of mass killings in Nazi-occupied Poland began with the invasion. On September 21, 1939, with a Nazi victory all but assured, the chief of the German Security Police, Reinhard Heydrich, sent the commanders of Nazi Germany's mobile killing units an urgent message. "Subject: Jewish Question in Occupied Territory." In this letter, Heydrich distinguished between a "final aim" for the Jews of Europe and the "stages leading to the fulfillment of this final aim." Part one of the letter demanded that all Jews be expelled from the Polish countryside and concentrated in cities like Warsaw and Łódź. In part two, Heydrich expressed the need in each Polish ghetto for a "Council of Jewish Elders" to be made up of "the remaining authoritative personalities and rabbis."

In Łódź, the Nazis chose a former orphanage director with a sordid reputation named Chaim Rumkowski. He had a mane of thick white hair and a notorious temper, and on October 13, 1939, a German commissar in Łódź "elected" Rumkowski to the position of council president and ordered him to appoint thirty-one members to the Jewish council, the *Judenrat*. Within one month, all of them were murdered, and once again, Rumkowski was ordered to select a group of men to join the *Judenrat*. This time, however, he was told to seek out more malleable beings, men who would be more likely to follow orders. How exactly the Nazis would use the *Judenräte* remained unclear to everyone, including most of the Nazi elite, but what wasn't a debate in the city of Łódź was Chaim Rumkowski's all-too-human desire for power.

Years before he became what historian Raul Hilberg called the Nazis' "indispensable operative," Rumkowski was a little-known director at the Helenówek Orphanage outside of Łódź. One day at the orphanage, Rumkowski made an urgent call to a certain Dr. Reicher and asked him to come to the orphanage to treat a few young girls for gonorrhea. Rumkowski insisted that he had no idea how the girls had contracted the venereal disease, speculating that perhaps it came from sharing dirty towels and sheets.

Dr. Reicher didn't ask any questions and treated the girls as best he could. He did, however, suggest sending the girls to a public clinic for further treatment, to which Rumkowski became agitated—tearful even, according to Dr. Reicher's post-war memoir, *City of Ash: A Jewish Doctor in Poland, 1939-1945*—and implored Dr. Reicher to treat the children privately at the orphanage.

Dr. Reicher complied, Rumkowski was relieved, and there was no further discussion of the incident. In November 1939, however, facing renewed orders to elect respected community members to the *Judenrat*, President Rumkowski called on his old acquaintance Dr. Reicher and berated him when the doctor refused to join the council. What follows is Dr. Reicher's testimony of that incident, and to the extent that any primary source can be trusted, Rumkowski's words are a matter of historical record: "You species of imbecile. Just what are you thinking? Do you think you can just do what you like? This is war, and we are like soldiers. We have to carry out orders, obey without condition and fulfill our tasks unconditionally—or die! If you do not do what I, the president of the Jewish Council, order, I will crush you like an ant. And if you, you shameless vermin, ever have the audacity to invoke our relationship at the orphanage, you will be sent to a place from whence no one returns alive!"

Viktor dreams of orange blossoms and elevator doors and a woman in red. He wakes up in the bitter cold, fully clothed, his shoes tied tight, his entire body tense like a knuckle that won't crack. Viktor hasn't been able to muster the courage to leave his apartment since Tadeusz and Joel's murders. He slept through the entire day he was supposed to report to the council offices, but if he doesn't go today, he could be responsible for the death of another friend.

Viktor is surprised to see Calel waiting in a ghetto police uniform at the council building entrance.

"Hello, my friend," Viktor says. "Is Henryk okay?"

Calel doesn't smile. "You're lucky there are no other translators. Henryk is with the president now. He'll be out shortly."

Calel leads Viktor into a small antechamber with barren walls and two wooden chairs. The frosted-glass door of the main office reads *Council of Jewish Elders President Chaim Rumkowski*, and opens to reveal Henryk Dawidowicz, the scar on his neck from the attack at the Astoria still visible.

Viktor embraces Henryk and holds back tears. "Tadeusz ..."

"Sasha, too. They raided the bakery."

Viktor pulls away. "What about Rachel and the children?"

"They weren't there," Henryk says. "Be smart now, Viktor. You must accept Rumkowski's offer. Now more than ever, the council needs good men."

"Henryk, you know where I stand—"

"Ah, is that Bauman?" Chaim Rumkowski's voice booms from the office. "Dawidowicz, I will see you for lunch in the canteen. Please, come in, Professor Bauman."

Viktor enters but refrains from taking a seat. Rumkowski's unkempt head of white hair makes him look both regal and mad.

"It's nice to finally make your acquaintance, professor. Please, sit down."

"Hello, Mr. Rumkowski. I won't be staying long."

"*President* Rumkowski, if you don't mind."

"Yes, Mr. President. I'm only here as a matter of courtesy to my friend Henryk. I'm afraid I'm not fit to be a council member, as I am sure he explained to you."

"Quite the contrary, professor. Dawidowicz tells me you're the perfect choice. You are of Jewish heritage, and you speak German. That is correct?"

"Yes, I speak German, but I've never observed Judaism, and I never knew my grandmothers."

Rumkowski smirks. "Are you ashamed of your heritage, Professor Bauman?"

"Not at all, Mr. President. My parents simply never passed down the faith."

Viktor remains standing as he scans the room's decorations: paintings of the Polish countryside, a framed Nazi decree, and a photo of children standing in front of an orphanage on Rumkowski's desk.

Rumkowski notices Viktor's eyes pause at the photo. "Ah, yes. My children in Helenówek. Such tender times. So, what will you have, Professor? Tea? Coffee? Please, have a seat."

"Nothing, thank you. I won't be long."

"Straight to business, I see. And a man of principle! It is an honorable trait, professor. Very well, then. As you know, you are Jewish according to the authorities, and that's good enough for me. I'm sure you are aware the community needs a German translator? I intend to make this community flourish. Do you understand?"

"Flourish?" Viktor doesn't hide his disdain. "Forgive me, Mr. President, but how can any community *flourish* inside a Nazi ghetto?"

"I have plans, professor, to do great things for this community. Some people are already calling me King Chaim."

"I heard a different name."

"Oh yes?"

'Yes. Chaim the Terrible."

Rumkowski forces a smile. "There will always be detractors, won't there? The weak-willed are envious of power, wouldn't you agree? This is why I am glad you have come to your senses. There will be many benefits and opportunities for devoted council members like yourself."

"Like I said, I'm only here out of respect for my friend."

"Careful, professor. Don't be simple. We all have to answer to someone. You don't have to agree with my position, but you will respect it."

"And it's quite the *position* you've found yourself in, Mr. President ... almost as impressive as your previous *accomplishments*."

Viktor nods at the photo of the orphanage.

Rumkowski's face turns crimson. "You species of imbecile, just what are you thinking? They're building a ghetto, and I have been put in charge. You speak German, I need a translator, and that's it. Finished."

"Is that a threat?"

"It is a fact."

"Well then," Viktor steps to the door. "I'm afraid you'll have to arrest me or find someone else. I'm not one of your orphans, Mr. President, and I have no interest in serving our oppressors."

Viktor hurries out of the building and knows better than to go home. Once around the corner, he picks up his pace. Every fiber in his being starts to burn as he hears the crunch of other footsteps closing in. He dashes down an alleyway and comes out to the other side, only to see in the distance a German patrol. He doubles back and ducks behind a large snowdrift on the boulevard. Looking over his shoulder, he sees a familiar silhouette approaching.

Viktor laughs in relief. "Ah, Calel, I thought I was done for."

"Professor," Calel's face is pale with fear. "Do *exactly* as I say."

Calel grabs Viktor's wrist and twists it behind his back. "Professor," Calel whispers, "they'll arrest me if I don't. I can help you, but I must take you to the police station. Please, just do exactly as I say. You're no good to anyone if you're dead, professor. Don't be stupid. I can save you from Gestapo interrogation."

Viktor smiles at Calel. "Calel ... Tadeusz, Sasha and Joel are dead, and I haven't seen Martin in days. Rachel and the children are missing, too. I will not join that council."

"Don't be a fool, professor. Don't die for nothing."

"It's not for nothing, Calel. This is about maintaining our humanity, our dignity."

"Survival is dignity, professor."

"Is that why you're having me arrested?"

Calel yanks Viktor back to the council offices, where a German policeman awaits

"Well? Is this our translator?"

"Please, Viktor. Just say yes," Calel whispers.

The officer snickers and hands Calel a wooden truncheon. "Beat him into submission."

Calel whimpers. "Please, Viktor."

"It's okay," Viktor lowers his head in preparation. "I forgive you."

Calel looks away as he raises the weapon with a trembling arm.

"Do it!" The policeman screams.

Calel drops Viktor with one blow to the side of the head.

"Again!" The officer yells. "Again! Now kick him!"

Crumpled on the ground, Viktor is amazed by how instinctively his body curls into a ball. He can hear Calel's sobs as the officer instructs the boy to keep striking, but Calel is weak, and his heart isn't in it. As Viktor's body is pummeled, he thinks of Tadeusz's last words—*"When you see my mother, tell her I said hello"*—and he envisions Rachel and the children safe in the countryside in the instant before the police officer takes Calel's baton and Viktor's world goes black.

Elsa is determined to get Viktor out of the city before the ghetto is sealed. She arrives at the office before dawn, but Frau Wolfmann is already there.

"What brings you in this early, Miss Dietrich?"

"Good morning, Frau Wolfmann. I'd like to request a company vehicle for a special task outside the city."

"Miss Dietrich," Frau Wolfmann snickers. "You know I can't allow that without proper documentation. Major

Brandt has to sign off on all vehicle authorizations."

Elsa's body is exhausted but her mind is awake, and she has no trouble lying these days, least of all to herself. "Frau Wolfmann. The major's health, as you know, is a priority of mine, and I'm concerned about his lingering cough. He's requested I contact a specialist in Berlin but has asked me to keep the specifics to myself. Of course, if you'd like to interrupt his work in the cellar—he's still down there, is he not?—and ask him why his *own personal secretary* needs a vehicle, then by all means, Frau Wolfmann," Elsa holds out her hands in snide supplication. "I'll wait for you here?"

Her callous tone earns Frau Wolfman's attention, if not respect.

Frau Wolfmann eyes Elsa suspiciously. "Something's changed in you. What is it? Have you met a man? You've been quite diligent, Miss Dietrich. I'm impressed with your work ethic. Very well then," she rummages in a desk drawer for the car keys. "Although far be it from me to question putting a young woman like yourself behind the wheel … really, it isn't proper. How did you even learn to drive? You can take one of the *Volkswagens* in the small depot, license plate WC-1942. It belongs to the auxiliary police unit. The schedule shows they won't need it until tomorrow morning. But you do understand, Miss Dietrich, that I will have to run this by the major?"

"I wouldn't expect anything less," Elsa forces a smile. "What time did he arrive this morning?"

"He never left. He's been down there all night."

"Very well. I'll prepare him some coffee before I leave." The amphetamines have made it easy for Elsa to feign her dutiful role. "Thank you, Frau Wolfmann, for respecting my position. I won't forget it. Have a good morning. *Heil Hitler.*"

Frau Wolfmann raises her eyebrows and smiles. "Yes, *Heil Hitler!* Perhaps Major Brandt was right about you. My reservations were misplaced. Do drive safely. And please do make sure it's back in the lot by tomorrow morning."

Elsa glides across the foyer and prepares Brandt's coffee in the kitchen. Over the past weeks, Brandt has been spending most nights in the cellar, which means Elsa's day begins before dawn to greet him with coffee when he emerges. She has few illusions about what's happening beneath her feet (they deliver the prisoners to the cellar via a back alleyway), which is why she's now crushing three Pervitins in Brandt's coffee. She can only imagine the effect of three: zero appetite, racing heartbeat, indifference to passing time, and extreme agitation and nausea through the night. Just one Pervitin per day has allowed her to finish her paperwork before lunch so she can spend her afternoons doctoring files of Jewish residents condemned to the ghetto—confusing addresses, changing names and birth dates, anything that might delay the process—but ultimately, Elsa knows regardless of her efforts, every single person the authorities deem Jewish will be sent to the ghetto by early May.

A sharp and sudden spasm of pain in Elsa's jaw causes her to knock a mug to the floor. She clenches her mouth and tries to massage away the ache in the space beneath her ear lobes.

Before cleaning up the mess and pouring Brandt's tainted coffee, she rubs a small amount of the leftover Pervitin on her gums and places Brandt's tray at the foot of his door. Down below, she can hear the faint sound of music playing.

She gets down on her knees and presses her ear to the floorboards; the unmistakable vibrations of Artie Shaw's "Begin the Beguine" seep up from the cellar, and then the tired cries and groans of tortured men pleading.

She hears footsteps coming up the iron stairwell and springs to her feet.

"Ah, Miss Dietrich. You're here earlier than expected," Brandt wipes sweat from his forehead. "Could you bring me the new prescription for my migraine? I cannot seem to shake whatever this is."

"Of course, Major Brandt. You look tired, sir. Let me handle the tray. I'll be there in a second."

Elsa shakes a single pill from a glass jar labeled Eukodal, a powerful opiate. The pharmacist warned her of combining these with amphetamines due to the potential strain on the heart—Elsa is counting on it.

"The pharmacist said this will help," she reassures him. "Frau Wolfmann tells me you've been working all night. What did I tell you about not taking any breaks?"

Brandt clutches his cup of coffee with two hands, like a child, and takes deep breaths between each sip. His face is paler than yesterday, but his forehead is gleaming with sweat. For the first time since Elsa has known him, Brandt appears weak.

"This is good, thank you," Brandt coughs violently into his handkerchief. A dark ring of sweat circles his unbuttoned neck collar. "When is the herbalist from Berlin arriving?"

"Soon," Elsa lies. There's no such thing as a Nazi-approved herbalist—Elsa simply invented him. "He's scheduled to travel to Warsaw later today, in fact."

"That is good news, Elsa. My mother always had the best herbal remedies."

This is only the second time Major Brandt has ever called Elsa by her first name.

"There's been an outbreak of Typhoid Fever in Bałuty," he says. "Do you think I could have caught it downstairs? Some of them are quite tough to crack, you know. Where did they learn to suffer so quietly? What did the pharmacist say about my condition?"

"The Eukodal should help with the jitteriness and the heart palpitations. What you need to do is rest, major. Take a few days off. All those hours in the cellar are killing you! You truly do exhaust yourself, sir."

Brandt heaves a sigh of relief. "Ah, Miss Dietrich, what would I do without you? Yet another excellent pot of coffee. I feel more awake already. I should probably get back down there, however."

Brandt rolls up his sleeves and dabs at his forehead with his translucent handkerchief. "In fact, why don't you take the rest of the day off? I'll be very busy downstairs today, and you're well ahead on the transcriptions. Take yourself to lunch at the Astoria, my treat. Put it on my name."

Elsa is amazed at her luck. "You're too kind, major," she feigns nonchalance. "And oh, by the way. The pharmacist was only able to give me the one Eukodal pill. There's a shortage here, and I need to go to Warsaw to pick up the rest. Could I take a car this afternoon?"

"Miss Dietrich, you spoil me. How did I get so lucky? Perhaps you could also inquire about the herbalist while you're there?"

"The herbalist?"

"Yes. The specialist you said is coming from Berlin."

"Ah, yes, of course! What a great idea, Major Brandt. We'll have you fixed up in no time."

Out in the motor pool of a half-dozen black *Volkswagens* blanketed in snow, Elsa finds license plate number WC-1942 and drives straight to Bałuty. She bangs on Viktor's door to no avail and drives through the neighborhood, asking if anybody has seen him. No luck. She tries knocking on Martin Arendt's door, too, but nobody is there. After another hour driving around, asking residents for any information, she decides to return home to rest.

"Would you like me to park the vehicle for the night?" The building's Nazi-approved concierge asks.

"No, thank you. I'll be going out later this evening. Just leave it out front."

Once upstairs, she pops another Pervitin—it's been twelve hours, after all—and opens a bottle of wine to quell her anxiety. After barely twenty-four hours in this apartment, her skin is already crawling. She is surrounded by stolen belongings in a building full of ghosts.

Elsa mists her orange blossom perfume in the corners of the room as some kind of purification ritual, especially around the gutted grand piano, and continues to suck from the bottle of wine. As the amphetamines take effect, she tries to understand what could have happened to Viktor. *Maybe he was caught during the raid at the bakery?*

A loud crash from up above shakes the ceiling light fixture, and now, the scurrying of childlike footsteps. Alert and curious, Elsa creeps up the flight of stairs and knocks lightly on the door.

"Please," Elsa speaks in Polish. "I want to help. My

name is Elsa."

She knocks softly but persistently until the door creaks open.

"I'm sorry for the noise," a woman's voice says from the obscurity. "We'll be quiet. Have a good evening, miss."

"No, please," Elsa wedges her foot in the door. Although the woman is barely more than a silhouette, Elsa swears she's seen her before. "I want to help. My name is Elsa Dietrich. Have we met?"

The door opens. "You are Viktor Bauman's friend."

"Yes, but how—"

"I saw you at the Astoria. They shot my husband and the man who lived downstairs."

"Of course ... you must be Rachel Sierakowiak?"

"Yes."

"Please, just listen. I can get you out of the city. It has to be tonight. Can I come inside? It's not safe not to speak in the corridor."

Rachel hesitates and looks Elsa in the eye. "What are you talking about?"

"I have a car. I can get us out of the city."

"That's ridiculous. There are checkpoints."

"Yes. And I have a Gestapo vehicle."

"What are you talking about?"

"I work for them, Rachel. I can get you out of here. But please, can I explain inside?"

Rachel breaks down in tears. Elsa hugs her and follows her down a hallway of broken glass, through a ransacked living room, and into a bedroom.

"We've been hiding here for two days," Rachel says.

"But our luck won't last the weekend. Where's Viktor?"

"I can't find him. I've been searching everywhere. That's why I wanted the car. They're going to seal the ghetto soon. I was sure I could find him before it's too late."

"You work for the Gestapo and you can't find him?"

"I'm just a secretary, Rachel. They tell me nothing. I'm only trying to help."

"Viktor was here in this building two days ago. Right where you're standing. They forced him to empty Joel's apartment and then they ... Tadeusz was covering our tracks ... we hid behind a ... Tadeusz sacrificed his life for us. I watched from the roof as they—wait, how did you hear us? You're not—"

Elsa lowers her head. "Yes. I am. They moved me in yesterday. Please, let me help you. We have to leave tonight."

Rachel walks to the large mahogany wardrobe in the corner of the room. "Children, it's okay. You can come out now."

Two small children crawl out from the wardrobe.

"Children, this is Elsa. She's Uncle Viktor's friend. She's going to get us out of the city tonight."

"Hello my little one," Elsa speaks to the little boy hiding behind his mother's legs. "And what's your name?"

"His name is Tadeusz," Rachel's voice shakes with heartbreak. "And this one is Ania. Can you get us to Wymagamówka? It's a few hours away. Tadeusz's mother is there. It's the only place we have."

"Can you be ready to leave in ten minutes?"

"Yes."

"Pack as lightly as you can."

Elsa returns to the lobby to ask the concierge to bring the car around, but he's no longer at his desk. Elsa calls out to him. She looks towards the entrance to see the concierge speaking to someone outside in the snowy gloom. A German policeman with a flashlight is inspecting the interior of Elsa's vehicle. Her stomach turns to knots when the policeman with the flashlight steps away: Carl's unmistakable, hulking silhouette floats in the space between two truck headlights.

Carl barges into the building with the concierge in tow.

"Miss Dietrich. I apologize. I didn't—"

"Hush," Carl snaps. "Good evening, Elsa." The stench of booze is heavy on his breath. "You're as pale as a ghost, darling. What is this I hear about you acquiring an authorized police vehicle? And to go to Warsaw, no less?"

The concierge steps in between Carl and Elsa. "I was trying to explain to Officer Becker that you have Gestapo clearance for the vehicle. Sir, I'm sure you're aware of SS-Major Brandt's specific needs. He wouldn't—"

"Keep your mouth shut," Carl shoves his truncheon into the concierge's throat. "Speak again and I'll have you arrested. Understand? I would like to speak to my fiancée in private."

"He's just doing his job," Elsa intervenes. "He's right, Carl. I need the car for official business.

"Bullshit. What kind of business, exactly?"

"None of your business," Elsa says, holding her ground. "I thought I told you to stay away from me."

Carl's drunken eyes pour over Elsa's body. She knows the look all too well. She saw it the night he threw her down the stairwell.

"Carl, if you wait for me here, we can talk upstairs when I return. But truly, my task cannot wait. It is a sensitive matter and a long drive to my destination, and I have to be back before dawn."

Carl laughs and grabs her wrist. "Oh, darling, well in that case, I think it's best I accompany you on your journey."

"Carl, please."

"I'm coming with you, Elsa. This isn't a debate. So what is this *special task?*"

Elsa responds instinctively. "I'm escorting a well-respected gentile family out of the city to make room for an SS officer in the building. A woman and her two children. They're ready to leave. Can I fetch them?"

During the drive, Elsa focuses on the faces of Rachel and the children in the rear-view mirror whenever Carl puts an unwelcome hand on her thigh. She doesn't speak to him once during the entire journey to Wymagamówka, and the passengers don't dare make a sound, either. Carl's presence has made a tense situation almost unbearable, but seeing the children in the mirror gives Elsa the strength to keep her terror at bay. *We're almost there.*

The black sedan's headlights slice through the country darkness until they come to a halt on a hillock in front of a house with a barn. A swinging lantern in the night greets them and the elderly caretaker escorts Elsa, Rachel and the children to the barn as Carl stays by the car, smoking and swigging from a large flask. Elsa knows he understands what's happening, but she also knows he's too drunk to care. In his inebriated state, lust always took priority.

Elsa accompanies Rachel, Ania, and Little Tadeusz

to the hayloft, where she leaves them with Wladyslaw, the caretaker, and promises she'll be back soon.

Rachel is agitated. "How could you bring *him* here? Won't he tell someone?"

"He has no idea where he is, trust me. I'm sorry, Rachel. I didn't have a choice. It's too long to explain, but I'll take care of him, don't worry. I'll try to come back soon and check on you."

"Don't try," Rachel takes Elsa's hand. "You'll come back with Viktor. You'll do it."

Elsa returns to Carl. On the drive back, she can feel his burning gaze on her neck, can hear him grinding his teeth like he always used to do in his sleep, can smell the stench of cigarettes and vodka on his breath. She tries to push his hand away from her as it inches towards her crotch, but Elsa focuses on the road and decides on a different strategy. "Be patient," she coos. "It'll be worth it, I promise."

It works. Carl soon dozes off, allowing Elsa to focus on her next steps, on the beaming headlights illuminating the speeding ground. Rachel and the children are now safe—she's done something tangible and real—and whatever price she has to pay is worth their survival. The rest is unimportant.

As searchlights appear and illuminate the night sky on the outskirts of Łódź.

Carl's vodka breath breaks the silence within the speeding vehicle with unwelcome words in Elsa's ear.

"Not here," Elsa's voice shakes. "I promise it'll be worth it. Just wait."

Once back on *Adolf-Hitler-Straße*, Elsa steps out of the vehicle and walks as slowly as she can, taking her time to hand the keys to the concierge, asking him questions that have no answers.

"Enough now. Let's go upstairs," Carl groans.

The red carpeting in the lobby burns bright from the chandelier's orange glare. Carl barks at Elsa from the stairway. She hesitates before ascending, hoping the concierge might somehow intervene, but what can he do?

Time slows to a crawl as she fumbles with her keys. When she enters her cold apartment she promises she'll be just a minute in the bathroom. From behind the locked door, she hears Carl undo his belt buckle and drop his pants to the floor. The last time she kept the door locked, he broke it down and beat her senseless. Elsa crushes up two Eukodal pills and snorts them in search of oblivion. Slowly, she turns the lock and steps out to face him.

Carl stands, grabs her throat, and slams her against the wall. Her whole body rings with the force of it, but thanks to the opiates, she feels little more than warm, violent pressure.

Elsa pleads with him. "Carl, please. You're drunk. Not like this."

"You think I'd let you get away with smuggling *Untermenschen* out of the city and not have you the way I want?"

As it's happening, Elsa is able to detach her mind from her body. She closes her eyes to acknowledge the good she's done for Rachel and the children. Maybe she can do the same for Viktor, and then, perhaps, even for herself.

Is it raining or is it bright out? Does nature take mind of a tragedy? Viktor cannot know, for he's being led underground, is thrown to the cold, hard earth with a violence his body hasn't learned to expect. He claws at the dirt floor as his eye adjusts to a dimly lit crypt. A kick to the stomach flips him onto his back, and another to his ribs sends Viktor's body slamming up against a stone wall.

From this crumpled vantage point, he takes in the sunken ceiling, a single light bulb dangling above. A guard with a boyish face pulls the light string, flicking it off and on again, scattering yellow light across the earthen cellar.

"Stay down, *Untermensch*," the young guard kicks Viktor in the face when he tries to sit up. Viktor floats in and out of consciousness as the guard beats him. By the time it's over, Viktor is coughing up blood, is surprised by the desperate pleading of his own voice. *Am I nothing more than an animal? I must be something more than this.* The pain is excruciating, but Viktor only has one choice. *You have to bear this.*

Viktor wakes up to the sound of his own desperate moans. His left eye is swollen shut and it takes great effort to keep the other open, but in this moment, Viktor is consumed by a far more pressing matter than sight: for the first time in his life, he's experiencing real hunger.

After countless hours in captivity, Viktor's body pools on the ground as it begins to consume itself. The stomach acid gnashes at his bowels. His head lolls from side to side, his arms and legs limp from the last beating, the whole of him overcome with inertia. As Viktor's good eye acclimates to the darkness, he sees half a dozen men sitting with their backs against the four walls of the cellar.

A whisper emerges. "Bauman? Is that you?"

Viktor doesn't recognize the voice and doesn't speak

lest he incriminate himself.

"Don't worry, professor. This is just to intimidate us. If they wanted us dead, they would've killed us already."

The standard laws of time do not apply in this cellar. The prisoners are of the earth now. Time is of no consequence. They are buried. The hunger and the hours play endless tricks on Viktor's senses as his shriveled stomach climbs up his sternum and gnaws at his esophagus. In his delirium, Viktor swears he can hear jazz music playing. At some point, the single swinging light bulb flickers on again, signaling a guard shift. Viktor watches a crumpled man on the far wall reach into his jacket and pull out a pocket watch. *Would knowing the time help? Would it help me bear this?* He sees the man with the watch hold up ten fingers just before the light is switched off. The ghostly image of ten fingers floating in space is what Viktor will come to remember. *Ten in the morning or ten at night? What would it change?* Viktor decides knowing the time is a good thing: it means life is still moving forward—progressing—*and if I can just make it another minute, another hour, this will soon turn into a day. Maybe somebody will bring me some water. Viktor, you can bear this.*

A hint of daylight appears at the top of the stairwell. *Is this salvation?* A pair of black boots, and then legs, and then a torso, and now the familiar boyish face of the guard. Whenever this particular one appears, someone is released. *Is this progress?* Whatever it means, Viktor's turn is coming.

The young guard pulls the light bulb string. "What are you looking at? Speak! Are you deaf? I asked you a question."

"Nothing," Viktor mutters. "I'm not looking at anything."

"Do you think this is easy for us?" There is fear in the guard's voice. He really says this: "It's not like I enjoy it, you know. It'd be much easier for me just to shoot you. I am clean before the bar of history. Future generations will congratulate me for my strength."

Viktor looks into the eyes of the young soldier and feels pity. "I'm sure it's not easy. No."

"You Jews think you're so much better than us," the boy is angry. "But you aren't. Dobrozyski! Stand now!"

The guard forces up the prisoner next to Viktor and punches him in the belly.

"This is your fault," the guard points at Viktor, grabs Dobrozyski by the hair, and drags him into the adjacent cellar.

Time begins moving faster.

Other men are snatched up for interrogation. "Wilnowski!" "Lipek!" "Zdanowicz!"

Each man prepares in silence and in different ways. One recites the Shema Israel, a faint whisper on his lips; another prays to Jesus; other men vomit; the man with the pocket watch holds up his hands each time there is light. *Nine o'clock. It's been at least twelve hours, perhaps an entire day.*

Viktor finds solace in the stillness and the imagined march of time, so that the thuds, slaps, and screams coming from the room next door become almost rhythmic, meditative. Some of the men are dragged out moaning, while others won't stop screaming, but most exit unconscious until the young guard standing at the door dumps a bucket of frigid water atop their heads.

Viktor knows better than to crawl towards the puddle to quench his thirst. The man with the pocket watch exits the interrogation room on his own two feet and whispers words of encouragement to Viktor: "Have faith. Be strong. Don't give up. You can bear this."

"Viktor Bauman!"

It's time.

"Piss yourself before you enter," a voice says from the darkness. "Do it now. Trust me."

Viktor is surprised at how much urine is still in his bladder. The warmth floods out of him. Viktor is thankful for the heat. When the guard lifts him, Viktor almost chuckles at the guard's disgust. Somehow, the stench is strangely invigorating. *You are still living and breathing. You can bear this.*

His eyes take time to adjust to the interrogation room's brightness. Two young guards force Viktor down into a wooden chair at a large wooden table.

"This one's been particularly difficult," the younger guard from the cellar says. Viktor catches his eye, and Viktor now realizes why he's been picking on him: this is the same quiet, dyslexic boy who used to sit in the back of the classroom in Viktor's history lectures. His name is Erich Müller, and each time Viktor would call upon him, Müller would clench his jaw in fear, just like he's doing now—only back then, he spoke with a stutter.

"Hello, Erich," Viktor says. "I'm glad to know your speech has improved."

Erich says nothing.

A high-ranking SS officer soon arrives and takes a seat across from Viktor at the long wooden table. The officer's lapels are covered in insignia, but what Viktor will remember most is the way the light in the cellar casts jagged shadows across his face.

The officer coughs, spewing a mist of sickness into the air. He's sweating profusely, and although his neck collar is unbuttoned, he's clearly having trouble breathing.

"*Bitte hinsetzen*," the officer says. "*Guten abend*, professor. My name is Major Brandt."

"*Guten abend*," Viktor replies.

"I have heard much about you," the officer continues in German as he unfolds a black leather pouch to reveal a collection of instruments: a corkscrew, a spatula, hammer and nails, and a silver spoon.

Viktor looks away.

"You are stoic, Professor Bauman."

"I'm no longer a professor," Viktor replies in Polish. "You can just call me Viktor."

A fist careens out of the white light into Viktor's right ear. The sound is all he experiences. The pain of a pierced eardrum will come later.

"You will answer me in German," Major Brandt says. "You are Austrian, after all. Aren't you, *professor*?"

"*Ich bin* Viktor Bauman," Viktor replies.

Another fist pummels the left side of Viktor's face. He holds onto the seat of his chair as the room begins to spin. Viktor's mind revolves around one thought: *they're only attacking your shell. You can bear this.* The thought is a revelation as another beating begins. *These men want to squash me like a bug, but I am not an insect. They can crack my shell, but they cannot break me.*

As Viktor's body is pummeled from all directions, he tries to detach his mind from his body. When the major takes the spatula to Viktor's throat, Viktor is amazed to think of his esophagus as something other, as nothing more than a canal of flesh and nerve endings connected to his spine—and isn't his spine just a swivel? A black cloth bag is thrown over Viktor's head and as the ringing in his ears slowly dissipates, he succumbs to a new kind of darkness, the sense that he is utterly alone. The darkness is all-encompassing, and when the adrenaline subsides, the pain sets in just as sure as the moans begin escaping his lips.

But somebody is still here. Or at least, Viktor can hear someone flipping through heavy pages in a book, and now the once-comforting sound of a pencil scribbling, and soon after, jazz music scratching into existence on a record player.

Viktor knows the tune. "Miss Otis Regrets" by Cole Porter. He once heard Mabel Mercer sing it in Paris, and for the most fleeting of instances, Viktor is transported to another time—a birthday weekend with Helen at the Ritz—but the hood comes off, and the blinding light returns, and through his blurry vision, Viktor can just make out Major Brandt prepping a syringe.

The sharp prick at the inside of Viktor's elbow precedes a warm sensation coursing through his veins.

"Breathe deeply, professor," the major says. "You might be wondering why I have given you a muscle relaxant. It is so that we can speak without any of the pain getting in the way. You will only be able to witness it. Isn't it incredible how the mind can detach itself from the body? You used to work as a psychiatrist in London. What was your role at the clinic, exactly, Professor Bauman?"

Viktor feels woozy. "I was the chief psychiatrist in the Department for Suicide Prevention."

"And what was your primary method of prevention?"

"We spoke to our patients and listened. We tried to help them find a sense of purpose."

"But that was not all you did. How many patients died during your psycho-surgical experiments?"

"They weren't experiments. They were a last resort for extreme cases."

"Answer the question."

"Three died."

"Out of how many?"

"Six."

"And what happened to the others, Professor Bauman?"

"They were never the same."

The muscles in Viktor's throat are too weak to swallow properly. His entire body feels like it's dripping to the floor.

Major Brandt smiles. "And you did this, ostensibly, to *help* their mental suffering? But instead, you killed three and destroyed the others. How can you justify such lamentable results, professor?"

Viktor's torturer stands, picks up a few rusty nails on the table, and holds them to the light for inspection. "Professor Bauman," he comes around the table to hold one of the nails up to Viktor's working eyeball. "Why would a psychiatrist focused primarily on non-invasive therapy result in such medieval practices to treat ... what was it you called it?" Major Brandt flips through a stack of papers. "Ah, yes. In your doctoral dissertation—Professor Henryk

Dawidowicz kindly provided me with a copy—you wrote, and I quote: 'severing certain connections in the prefrontal lobe appears to assuage the patient's crisis of existence. Though rendered docile, the lobotomy provides the patient with a euphoric tranquility.'"

"We were wrong," Viktor winces with a different kind of pain, but the relaxants do nothing to erase the memory of Helen. "We erased their humanity."

"But you were onto something, weren't you?" Major Brandt dangles a piece of paper in front of Viktor's face. "It says it right here, in your conclusion: 'future research must investigate those areas in the prefrontal lobe that specifically deal with the creation of purpose and meaning.' This is quite the revolution, professor. I must say, I'm intrigued."

"It was barbaric," Viktor closes his good eye.

"Ah! Barbarism. Yes … I'm sorry I was never able to attend that lecture. But where is barbarity located in the human brain? You were scheduled to speak on it, weren't you, with Professor Dawidowicz? 'It is a peculiar fact,' you wrote, 'that modern societies have not done away with, but rather found justification for, humanity's most barbaric inclinations. Perhaps cruelty is not, in fact, antithetical to the human condition, but rather the other side of the civil coin.' Fascinating thoughts, professor. And I completely agree! To be cruel is to be human. But I would take it one step further: it is a necessity because, without cruelty, we have chaos."

Viktor shakes his head. "That's not what I—"

"We are not so different, you and I, professor. Never before in our history have we reached such heights, and never before in history have we witnessed such wickedness.

Do you know why you're here, Professor Bauman?"

"I'm still searching for that answer."

"Allow me to enlighten you. You are here because you were meant to be. As a physician in Berlin, I spent many years studying these very same questions, and here you are, a German-speaking half-breed from Austria with a degree in psychiatry, sitting right in front of me. Professor Bauman, this is destiny! But what I would like to know is this: if there is a location in the human brain designed for the creation of meaning and purpose, does it not stand to reason that there is *also* a location in the human brain designed for *destruction*? And if this is true, could we not cut out *that part* as well? Could we not eradicate the very idea of Judeo-Bolshevism, for example, with such a procedure?"

Viktor's entire body is now numb from the injection. "Ideas cannot be destroyed."

"Well, we can start by eradicating the people who harbor them. With time, ideas can be buried."

Major Brandt expels a guttural cough and shudders at the sight of what he's spit into his handkerchief. "Let's use you for example. Both of your grandmothers were Jews, which makes you the *ideal* candidate for a respectable position on the council."

Major Brandt walks over to the record player and turns up the volume to the haunting melody of "Stardust" by Hoagy Carmichael.

"So, what do you say, professor? Agree to join the council right now, and you will walk out of here on your own two feet. Alternatively..." Major Brandt holds the nail up to Viktor's eye. "Let's see how that clever brain of yours makes sense of me driving this nail through your hand before I move on to my other instruments."

Viktor tries to speak, but his mouth won't move. He couldn't obey Brandt's demands if he wanted to, and his torturer knows this.

Major Brandt smiles. "Very well. Guards, tie him to the chair and leave us be."

The two guards use a thick rope to bind Viktor's limp body to the chair. With his one good eye, Viktor watches Major Brandt slide on a pair of leather gloves. *You are more than an insect. You might not even feel it. Whatever happens, just remember: he can only crack your shell.*

The guards pull Viktor forward and splay his hands out on the wooden table. In the moment before the hammer falls, he notices dozens of nails stuck in the table, glistening with blood. He steels himself.

You can bear this, Viktor.

Viktor, you can bear this.

meaning

"If we have our own why of life, we shall get along with almost any how."

—Friedrich Nietzsche, *Twilight of the Idols*, 1889

In a Yale University basement in July 1961, a psychologist named Stanley Milgram set out to understand how ordinary people can commit mass murder. Given the right circumstances, Milgram believed most people would inflict pain on their fellow human beings due to peer pressure and obedience to authority.

The test involved three protagonists: the Teacher, the Learner, and the Authority. The Teacher and the Learner sat on opposite sides of a wall while the Authority, wearing a white lab coat, instructed the Teacher to ask the Learner a series of questions. The Teacher sat in front of a large machine called the Shock Generator, which had a series of switches ranging from 15 to 450 volts. Beneath those numbers were descriptors ranging from "slight shock" to "severe shock." If the Learner incorrectly answered one of the questions, the Authority instructed the Teacher to electrocute the Learner with increasing intensity.

The results astonished Milgram: 65% of all Teachers followed the Authority's orders until the near-fatal electroshock; although the Learners were only actors pretending to be electrocuted, Milgram's conclusion was a watershed moment in the history of the humanness of cruelty: "If a system of death camps were set up in the United States, one would be able to find sufficient personnel for those camps in any medium-sized American town."

Seven years later, the day after Martin Luther King Jr. was assassinated, a schoolteacher in Iowa named Jane Elliott set out to teach her students about bigotry. On the morning of April 5, 1968, she told all her brown-eyed students that they were better than the blue-eyed ones. Within hours, the brown-eyed children became arrogant, bossy, and bigoted. The next day, Elliott reversed the roles, telling the blue-eyed students that they were in fact superior, and while the blue-eyed children did take a certain pleasure in their newfound superiority, their prejudice was less pronounced, for they'd already experienced the effects of discrimination.

What's most surprising about our ability to be cruel towards each other is that it continues to surprise us. In August 1971, at Stanford University, just one month after *The Pentagon Papers* revealed the USA's brutal bombing campaign in Laos, Cambodia, and Vietnam, which killed hundreds of thousands of civilians, a psychologist named Philip Zimbardo set out to understand how ordinary people's behavior might change when placed in positions of power.

Zimbardo built a makeshift prison in a Stanford University basement and selected two groups of volunteers: Guards and Prisoners. Within days, Zimbardo realized the prison simulation was "a sufficient condition to produce aberrant, anti-social behavior." Zimbardo himself became megalomaniacal, refusing to shut down the project until an assistant professor named Christina Maslach persuaded him to stop the experiment (one year later, they were married). "Most dramatic and distressing to us," Zimbardo concluded, "was the observation of the ease with which sadistic behavior could be elicited in individuals who were not sadistic 'types.'"

Humanity's innate fascination with purpose and power can manifest as both empathy and cruelty. Because while it's comforting to use words like "right" and "wrong" and "righteous" and "monstrous," the truth is these words are the real fictions of history. The belief in these myths, in "purity," "sanctity," "Good" and "Evil" is the hallmark of self-righteous bigotry, for these words are defined less by what they are than by what they are not.

The bigot looks outward instead of within, forever gazing away from himself. The bigot is trapped in this hatred of "the other," for he cannot imagine existing without an enemy. The bigot cannot conceive of fluidity because, like all fundamentalists, the bigot lacks imagination. His identity depends upon opposition, which is why the bigot's dreams are limited to censorship and destruction.

Inevitably, the bigot becomes obsessed with the very thing he despises. Unable to create, he relies on an enemy to destroy and is thus regressive by definition, obsessed with an impossible future defined by a mythical, violent past. In the bigot's worldview, doctrines, philosophy, and even architecture follow suit, for the bigot's laws reveal less about what he stands for than what he fears.

Without total control, his project falters. By representing the enemy as a robber, the bigot becomes a victim of a robbery; by defining the enemy as dirty, the bigot becomes clean; by representing the enemy as Evil, the bigot justifies cruelty in the name of Good. But the bigot's existence is doomed from the start for the same ontological reason as the parasite's: the bigot can only exist so long as he remains attached to a healthy host.

Elsa brushes her teeth and gargles salt water and takes a scorching shower after Carl's third visit in as many nights. She has no illusions anymore—she's trapped again—but at least she was able to save Rachel and the children. But was it enough? She has to do more to make sacrificing her body seem worthwhile. The date has been set for the sealing of the ghetto, and after April 30, 1940, it will be impossible for Elsa to help Viktor escape, which is why she's taking a car into the ghetto to try and find him before it's too late.

Carl can't wait to get home to Elsa. His unit will soon be responsible for guarding the ghetto wall, which means Carl can call *Litzmannstadt* (and finally Elsa) his home.

Elsa hasn't agreed to let him move in yet, but all in good time. Carl was elated by her willingness to have him three nights a week in exchange for the occasional use of a battalion vehicle, and even if he knows she's using it to visit those *Untermenschen* out in the country, being with Elsa makes it worth it, makes him feel alive. He hasn't been this happy since Hamburg, or perhaps even since Danzig, when his mother was still alive, and long as he's patient and goes easy on the vodka, sooner or later Elsa will come around. He's sure of it.

Security around the ghetto's perimeter is increasing daily, with armed guards patrolling the outer walls and multiple watchtowers that have been erected along the firebreak, a desolate no man's land between the ghetto and the rest of the Nazified city. Gnarled barbed wire lines the top of the brick wall, with more spools of wire lying in wait to be stretched across the firebreak. Major Brandt showed Elsa the blueprints the other night. "It will be the second largest ghetto in the Empire, second only to Warsaw. But *Litzmannstadt* will have something even Warsaw does not: total separation. Not a single Aryan in this city will ever have to come in contact with an *Untermensch* again."

Elsa comes to a halt at the main ghetto entrance, where two red-faced guards waddle towards her with hungry eyes. They jeer and grab their crotches and champion the impressiveness of their genitals.

Elsa sneers and pulls out her party card. "Clearly, you're both new here, so I'll make this brief. I work for SS-Major Brandt." Elsa hardly recognizes her voice, uttering these words with such arrogance. "So perhaps you'd like to start by giving me your names and ranks?"

The men's faces drop as they step away from the vehicle.

Elsa makes a show of pulling out a black ledger and a pen. "Well? Your names? The Major will be very upset to know I was kept waiting."

"I'm nobody."

"What's that?"

"Nobody," the other one says.

"Precisely. You're nobody. So why don't you make

yourself useful and fetch me whatever documents you have detailing the ghetto council's administration buildings? Don't keep me waiting."

One of the guards scurries to a striped guard house and returns with a typewritten page detailing the *Judenrat's* extensive bureaucracy. The Central Office sits at the top of the pyramid, lording over nearly a dozen departments: Food Supply, Department of Kitchens, Finance and Economy Division, Gas Bureau, Purchasing Office, Ghetto Bank, Central Workshops Bureau, School Department, the Ghetto Police, which includes the Jewish Order Service, known as the OD (*Ordnungdienst*); a Special Section (*Sonderabteilung*) tasked with the search and seizure of concealed valuables; a Detective Department, the Department of Sanitation Control, and finally Elsa finds what she's looking for, the ghetto's Central Prison, but there's no address.

"Where's the central prison located?"

"It hasn't been built yet."

"So where are they putting prisoners?"

"I'm sorry, madame. I really can't say. I'm just a sentry."

"So you're useless."

"Y-yes, madame. Perhaps the Central Office would know—"

"Just open the gate."

Elsa returns to her vehicle. The thawing winter ground cracks and squelches beneath the tires as she rolls through the ghetto's desolate streets, trying to find anyone lingering outside who might be willing to speak to her or divulge any information. No luck. The few people she sees in the streets scurry away at the sight of her vehicle, and as the sun begins to set, Elsa realizes the absurdity of attempting to speak to ghetto residents in a German police vehicle just minutes before curfew.

When she arrives back home at *Adolf-Hitler-Straße*, she notices all the lights are on in her apartment. This is supposed to be her night off, but Carl is waiting.

"Miss Dietrich! Where have you been?" Brandt's chauffeur is waiting in the lobby. "There's been an emergency. Major Brandt had a stroke. He's currently in hospital. The surgeon is on his way."

Elsa cracks a smile, which confuses the chauffeur. "Would you like to inform your fiancé of the situation? He was quite agitated when I told him you'd be needed back at the office immediately."

"No, that's quite alright. Let's go see the major."

When the body experiences pain, there's an expectation of salvation. In moments of great terror, it is all too human to scream out for help. Such an assurance that someone or some *thing* will save us is fundamental to the human condition, but for Viktor Bauman, down in the Gestapo cellar beneath the cold earth of Bałuty, clinging to this kind of hope would have only sharpened the torturer's blades.

Down in the cellar, Viktor had no illusions that a savior would break down the door. Instead, he did his best to grit his teeth and bear it. Buried somewhere within the unexamined corners of his mind was the assumption that human beings are basically decent, but once they nailed the loose skin of his elbows to the wooden table, contorting his entire body into submission, Viktor learned that his belief in humanity could just as easily be weaponized against him.

Down there, Viktor learned that the virtues of kindness, empathy, and mutual respect are not a given, and in fact require remarkable effort. Down there, Viktor learned that some people find more meaning taking the blunt edge of a silver spoon to a man's eye than in showing mercy. Beneath the earth, Viktor learned that family men who have pets and small children are capable of casually standing by while a tortured professor's former student can, in the name of duty, pull down his teacher's trousers and insert sharp objects into his rectum. Underground, Viktor's illusion of being safe within his own body was obliterated … and oh, how beautifully childish he'd been to have placed such blind faith *in anything* for so long, let alone the idea of a categorically positive definition of the human condition.

Salvation came when he understood no one would save him. It came from within, from the remote corners of his mind, where Viktor learned that while, yes, his head and his elbows and his ears and his testicles were a part of him, they were not his essence; yes, he was something more than a collection of bones and organs in loose skin; his body was nothing more than a vehicle, an appendage, and the *why* of the pain became proof that he was still alive, so that he could steady his mind with the memory of sitting on a terrace once again, or of a lazy summer day with Martin at the Astoria Café, or of the possibility of seeing Elsa on a terrace again. In the contemplation of these beloveds, Viktor was able to exist elsewhere, if only momentarily … and what a relief those moments were to realize that yes, he, Viktor Bauman, had a reason to bear this.

Afterward, sitting dumbfounded against the stone wall

in the adjacent cellar, Viktor proceeded to touch his face and survey his fingers, arms, and legs, amazed to realize that, yes, he still had a forehead and that, yes, his nostrils could still expand and contract, and that, yes, he still had a mouth and a working tongue. His left eye, too, would see again, if only barely, and his trachea would one day produce language and even laughter, somehow.

Days of recovery will turn into weeks. Viktor will remain semi-conscious in bed until, eventually, his eye socket will stop bleeding, and the vision will return. After a month in traction, once the ghetto has been sealed, Viktor will try walking to the bathroom on the landing without a cane and he will fail. When Martin cannot be with him, Viktor will navigate the world of his apartment by grasping his only supports—a bedside table, a lamp, the wall, the edge of his desk—and the day he makes it to the kitchen without stumbling will feel like a tremendous victory. But then, on a hot day in May, 1940, Viktor will contract Typhoid Fever. Fearing that his friend is on the brink, Martin will call a doctor who works for Rumkowski's council. After the medicine takes effect, Viktor will learn that if he's alive, it's because he's now a *Judenrat* member, and once he's well enough to work ("take your time," Henryk will say), Viktor's job will be translating documents for the council's Department of Statistics.

In the subsequent weeks, Viktor will go through the five stages of grief. He will falter at step four, depression, and will search for answers in books of psychiatry and philosophy, underlining ideas about paradoxical intention and sublimation. Viktor will learn to focus on the small things: the cups of tea and the early mornings spent with his book collection, playing chess with Martin, a ghetto piano recital, walking along the firebreak. Later that summer, Viktor will imagine a world where Elsa Dietrich might still be sitting at an elegant café terrace, and Viktor will even start writing again—short poems, fleeting ideas, unambitious stories, incomplete essays—and in all of these small ways, slowly, he will approximate acceptance.

hope

"When the sun shines, my mood is lighter. How sad life is. When we look at the fence separating us from the rest of the world, our souls, like birds in a cage, yearn to be free. Longing breaks my heart, visions of the past come to me."

—Anonymous Diarist, Łódź Ghetto, 1942

What is the color of forgetting? A cosmic black hole? A blinding white light? Or is it the phantasmagoria of colors we see when we press our palms to our eyelids and keep applying the pressure?

Despite our best efforts to understand it, to control it, to chase it down, time eludes us. Sometimes, it comes at us slowly, measured; other times, it happens all at once. We eat the Madeleine, we hear the train whistle, we get a phone call from the police, and we're transported to another time. A decade can seem like a fleeting memory. A single minute on the telephone can seem like a lifetime. Small details— the sound of a tea kettle coming to a boil, the crackle of firewood in autumn, the scent of an old lover's perfume in a crowded street—can feel as expansive as the cosmos, while vast plains of our daily existence hum quietly beneath the surface.

We always think we have more time. We tell ourselves we'll write the next chapter tomorrow, call our mother next week, and finish the manuscript next year. Nothing happens until, suddenly, a historic event comes careening at us, forcing us to remember where we've come from and where we want to go.

"We noticed significant atrophying in the hippocampus, but also in the frontal lobe," the doctor told me on the phone. "There are some issues with her protein deposits that suggest neurodegeneration ... did your mother experience any personality changes before her fall?"

In retrospect, yes. My mother had become a bit more aggressive—agitated even. She'd started showing signs of confusion about a year before the foreclosure: she would take wrong turns on drives she'd done hundreds of times and would put on the tea kettle without any water in it. She'd accuse friends of moving objects around the house, too. The doctor's diagnosis was FTD—frontotemporal dementia. It was aggressive, he said. "It's good that you called."

My mother knew something was wrong the moment I hung up the phone. Her reaction wasn't disbelief so much as resignation, a dreaded truth she'd spent years ignoring as her mother wilted away in an Alzheimer's facility. I tried to reassure her we could fight it together, and for the first time in many years, we were a united front. During that first month after her diagnosis, we attended academic lectures at local universities about neuroplasticity and psychedelic therapy, listening to countless stories about how tragedy can be transformed into triumph. We spent afternoons listening to books on tape: Jill Bolte Taylor's *My Stroke of Insight*, Norman Doidge's *The Brain that Changes Itself*, and

Michael Pollen's *How to Change Your Mind.* We learned about Positive psychology, Cognitive behavioral therapy, and educated ourselves on the human brain's ability to adapt and heal itself.

The day before my departure, my mother and I were speaking in the kitchen of her new apartment. The kitchen was my favorite room as a child, that liminal space between two worlds, just before the dinner ritual began. It was always there where we bonded most during my childhood—tea in the morning, a snack in the afternoon, cooking dinner together—which is why it felt fitting to reveal to her in her new space that my book about history, memory, and the Nazi Occupation of Poland was also about her and my childhood. This time, I was the one telling her there was something she needed to remember.

The story of life in the Łódź Ghetto can only ever really be told by the people who lived it. Ghetto diarists like Josef Zelkowicz and Dawid Sierakowiak, both murdered by the Nazis, told the story far better than any historian or author ever could. The prewar Jewish population of Łódź was almost two hundred thousand; fewer than 10,000 were alive by the end of the war. When the ghetto was sealed on April 30, 1940, it contained just under 164,000 people, mostly Jewish people and a small Roma population. When the Soviet Army liberated the ghetto on January 19, 1945, they found only 877 survivors.

Still, despite the terrible odds, seasons came and went on both sides of the wall. In the spring of 1940, flowers blossomed, as did Typhoid Fever and dysentery. The Nazi side of the city, renamed *Litzmannstadt* in honor of a dead

German general, had open-air markets with fresh produce, a water park, plans for a new sports stadium, and
even a zoo. In Helenenhof Park, which still exists, I know
there was an enclosure filled with lions and tigers and ele-
phants. What I don't know is what it must've been like to
hear an elephant trumpet from the other side of the wall.
It must have made the nightmare of the ghetto that much
more surreal to imagine a petting zoo just a few kilometers
from the muddied streets and infected bowels of Bałuty.
The historical record also tells me that to create a buffer
between the Łódź Ghetto and *Litzmannstadt*, the Nazis
built firebreaks—windswept fields covered in weeds and
barbed wire—to separate the two worlds and deter smugglers. From their guard towers, German snipers surveyed
the firebreak while vicious dogs and their masters patrolled
down below. I know that smugglers risked their lives each
day transporting essential foodstuffs and medicine to help
friends and family survive just one more day, and while I
wonder if any of those men up in the guard towers ever
wrote a love letter to their family, I'm haunted by the unde-
niable truth that a human being tasked with shooting children on sight can also write sweet nothings to the mother
of his children.

I'm haunted by something else: in the summer of 1940,
newly arrived German migrants went to the lakeside outside
the city, and while I know the air was fresh on their side of
the wall, I imagine the occasional odor of death still wafted
into those long summer days, perhaps even caught flight on
the breeze all the way to the lakeside, where willfully igno-
rant sunbathers squinted their eyes in denial, pretending
their pleasure had nothing to do with others' pain. I know
the Nazis built a tramway to facilitate weekend outings,

and I can almost hear the bourgeois commuters complaining about the stench as the tram rolled past the ghetto. I can also imagine a little boy asking his mother about the smell, simultaneously curious and terrified of what existed on the other side of "civilization." I can imagine this because during this period, the Nazis organized a sweeping tourism campaign for the "City of the Future," welcoming busloads of Hitler Youth to *Litzmannstadt*; famous German photographers hired by a local newspaper, *The Lodscher Zeitung*, even produced a travel feature in March 1940. In it, the writer describes how the Third Reich's sworn enemies have disappeared overnight and "woe to the criminals should they ever dare show their faces here again."

Weeks later, a documentary film crew of artists and intellectuals traveled to *Litzmannstadt* to highlight the state-of-the-art water park and the manicured boulevards of *Adolf-Hitler-Straße* and *Herman-Goring-Straße*, where they captured smiling children at *Deutschlandplatz* and ethnic Germans flocking to the new opera house on grainy film. These documentary artists used expensive lighting and cutting-edge cameras to film the city's stadium and renovated municipal pool, and on the outskirts of the city, along the gentle currents of the river Ner, the cameramen focused on bucolic images of rolling countryside and low-hanging trees. But I wonder how much they truly believed in Hitler's deranged vision of a utopian metropolis—was it as simple as changing a few street names to conjure the fairy tale? Polish streets were erased to make room for Little Red Riding Hood Alley, Cinderella Street, The Seven Dwarves' Passage, and Hansel and Gretel Way. Yes, these street names really did exist, as did the thoroughfares of Handel, Wagner, Mozart, and Schubert. The travel documentary was called *From Łódź to Litzmannstadt*, and though I want to believe that everyone who worked on that film felt guilty, how often do people feel guilty in a "civilized" society which tells them they're not doing anything wrong?

When they filmed the other side of the wall, the filmmakers focused on reflections of dilapidated buildings in dirty puddles, zooming in on shallow footprints in muddied streets, further "proof" that the "subhumans" did not belong in "their" city. I know they did this to create the illusion of just how far the "City of the Future" had come, but I wonder how they convinced themselves that their work in *Litzmannstadt* was a testament to the height and not the nadir of human civilization. Because the questions on this side of the wall were different: "Will I have to stay behind this barbed wire forever?" asked an anonymous Łódź Ghetto diarist. "Will there always be a booth with a German guard who has a rifle on his shoulder? Has it always been like this? Will it stay like this? Oh, no! But who is going to live through it? I miss freedom."

In the summer of 1941, when *Judenrat* President Chaim Rumkowski was faced with the coming reality of deportations, he and his council members had to make the terrible choice of who to condemn. Many believed in Rumkowski's "rescue through work" policy, which transformed the ghetto into one of Nazi Germany's most valuable labor camps; many others dismissed Rumkowski as a profiteering despot. When the deportations to Chelmno began in earnest in early 1942, however, all forms of logic and politics changed. On March 1, there were 142,079 people in the ghetto. One month later, 115,102 remained. But how many ghetto residents understood the council's impossible predicament, and how many knew how much Rumkowski invested in soup kitchens, hospitals, orphanages, and public works projects? And would it matter if we learned the precise number of people who spoke of President Rumkowski as "King Chaim" versus "Chaim the Terrible?" Both names speak to truths and falsehoods. To reject either transforms history into a fable.

Alas, all we can do is look at the historical record and study the works of historians like Isaiah Trunk, Raul Hilberg, Jacob Robinson, and Hannah Arendt. Because herein lies yet another haunting truth: on a hot summer day on June 13, 1941, the bespectacled leader of the SS, Heinrich Himmler, arrived in Bałut Market in a green BMW convertible with the license plate SS-I. Ghetto policemen stood guard around Himmler's convoy of six vehicles. According to a local source, the female secretaries in Rumkowski's office were dressed as if "for a ball." There is photographic proof of President Rumkowski wearing a Panama hat, a smile, and white gloves as he stands beside Himmler's car. So what did ghetto residents think when they saw the ghetto police guarding a Nazi motorcade in Bałut Market? And what did Rumkowski say to Himmler as he sat in the passenger seat of his BMW? Did Rumkowski believe Himmler's visit was a sign of better times to come? And when the first major deportations to the Chelmno killing center began in January 1942, why did Rumkowski say of the first deportees, "When I am deporting all kinds of connivers and cheats, I do it fully convinced that they asked for this fate."

I don't have the answers to these unanswerable questions—such is the nature of history—but I do know that whether considering the words of Heinrich Himmler or the anonymous Łódź Ghetto diarist or President

Chaim Rumkowski's "Give Me Your Children" speech of September 4, 1942, to explain is not to excuse and to understand is not to forgive.

Such is the complexity of human nature, of perpetrators, victims, and bystanders: those who have a Why can bear or commit almost any How.

Late March, 1942. Zero degrees outside and not much warmer within. Viktor is beginning to wonder if this winter will be his last. Whenever a heavy snow freezes the water pipes, Viktor burns his books to keep the apartment heated. Viktor keeps a list of all he's destroyed and promises to rebuild his small library if he can somehow survive this war: 253 books in total since emerging from the Gestapo cellar in the spring of 1940; this winter's ledger details twelve books burned in January, thirteen in February, and four by the Ides of March.

At the Jewish Council's Department of Statistics, Viktor continues translating various documents from German to Polish. He's now also responsible for overseeing the translation of renewed deportation lists; becoming a part of the machinery of destruction is the only reason he hasn't been killed. He's learned to keep his head down—survival is his act of resistance—and although his shame and anxiety manifest in frequent trips to the bathroom, long bouts of silence, and many sleepless nights, Viktor has learned to place his faith in small victories: in the cleaning-up of dirty dishes and tidying an unmade bed; in trimming his toenails; in drinking smuggled tea with Martin; in the small, sacred rituals that remind him of his humanity.

Martin was forced out of his home and into Viktor's ghetto apartment last autumn. Most of the 25,000 people deported into the ghetto in late 1941 have been crammed into one-room apartments around the deteriorating Bałut Market. Still, despite Viktor's rotting ceiling, the black mold beneath the kitchen sink, the cracked living room window, Viktor and Martin are lucky to have a space to call their own.

Tonight, they're huddled in hats and gloves around the lingering warmth of Viktor's potbelly stove. They lap at their bowls of watery gruel—to call it soup would be delusional—and Viktor pinches his nose with one hand and spoons the anemic liquid with the other lest he get a whiff of the rotten cabbage.

Viktor looks at his ailing friend with hollow eyes. Martin has lost his fat belly and the rest of his hair, and his back is more hunched than ever. He also suffers from daily headaches and chronic diarrhea, and though he coughs and snores through the night, Viktor is thankful not to be alone. Viktor's body began resisting him the day he was finally coerced into accepting a job at the *Judenrat's* Department of Statistics. The council doctor attributes Viktor's chronic pain to malnutrition, which might also explain the rash on his stomach, forever red and angry, and his rickety bones and joints that clink like the scaffolding holding up the ghetto bridge.

Martin offers Viktor the bed tonight, says he'd like to be closer to the front door incase he needs to use the bathroom. He curls up on the floor and pulls a lice-ridden blanket over his head. As a textile factory worker, Martin leaves the apartment each morning at 4 a.m. to avoid walking alongside the horse-drawn sewage carts that leave at dawn.

Viktor has witnessed these festering transports overloaded with human waste get stuck in the snow and the mud, spilling their slop on the way to the edge of the ghetto. The stench fills the air with tuberculosis, cholera, and dysentery, and though Martin knows to cover his nose and mouth on his commute, with each morning comes a renewed risk of infection.

Martin is already snoring, but Viktor is tormented by thoughts of the large Czech family (six adults and four children) living in Mrs. Eberhardt's old apartment. Viktor has been smuggling food out of the council canteen for months now, but this won't save them if the latest deportation rumors are to be trusted: the next trains are coming for all of the children under ten. The ghetto's population swelled when Western European Jews were sent in. There remain over 140,000 human beings in the Łódź Ghetto, and President Rumkowski says what matters most is prioritizing healthy, productive factory workers.

In response to the overcrowding, social Darwinism has flipped traditional morality on its head: non-Polish women, children, sick, and elderly are the last to be spared. Viktor listens to Martin's labored breathing and wonders how long they have left. The more recent deportees being held in the ghetto come from everywhere and nowhere, seemingly appearing overnight speaking Polish, Dutch, Yiddish, German, Romanian, Hungarian, and Czech (Viktor even once heard French).

An oppressive, all-too-human form of social hierarchy has developed in the council offices, too. President Rumkowski has vowed to protect "his Jews"—the Polish ones—first. He then favors Western Europeans for unknown reasons, and rumor has it that most of the

Central and Eastern European families will soon be sent to labor farms "further east," but few believe vegetables grow in the darkness of a Soviet winter.

Viktor hides his head under his pillow to quell these thoughts and the whispers of a darker premonition of a labor camp called Chelmno (on official documents, he translates the name to the German *Kulmhof*, outside of the Nazified town of *Warthbrücken*). The rumors arrived with a frantic traveler from Warsaw ~~who really did exist~~ who managed to smuggle himself into the Łódź Ghetto to warn the council. President Rumkowski refused to give the traveler an audience, but Viktor, Henryk, and a few others took him outside to listen to his tall tales about a place called Chelmno. The traveler swore he'd witnessed hundreds of Jews, Poles, and Roma being gassed in diesel trucks whose exhaust pipes were converted to pump fumes back into the sealed compartment. With crazed eyes, the man fell to his knees and broke down in tears, desperately trying to explain the existence of gas vans operating in the forest near Chelmno. As a crowd began to gather around the increasingly hysterical man, many jeered at him, called him a lunatic, and scolded him for scaring the children. The ghetto police soon arrived and dragged him away. Within minutes, a Nazi bureaucrat with kind eyes and a toothy smile arrived to quell the anxious crowd, insisting that while, yes, there was a labor camp outside of Koło, it "comfortably housed 100,000 farmers, all of them safe and sound and warm, all of them doing good work for those in the ghetto factories. Do not worry yourselves or jeopardize your safety by believing in such ridiculous rumors."

There was no more talk of the traveler from Warsaw, but Viktor's memory of the man's terrified conviction lingers tonight. Who in their right mind would smuggle themselves *into* the Łódź Ghetto to peddle such hysteria? And what is a gas van? It sounds too absurd to be made up. Then again, why would they be killing thousands when the ghetto factories are more productive than ever? Reality is ceasing to make sense.

Viktor hardly sleeps. Today, President Rumkowski is giving a celebratory speech at a textile factory. Viktor arrives in a large warehouse and takes a seat next to Henryk at a long wooden table of thirty-something chairs with Rumkowski at the head. The council president wears a thick, luscious coat with a velvet collar and smiles at his new wife by his side and at his secretary, Dora Fuchs, and then at the head of the ghetto police, Leon Rozenblat, whose stern mouth doesn't reciprocate the gesture. Behind Rumkowski is a gigantic portrait of the president himself, and a huge banner that reads "Work Is Our Only Path."

"What is happening?" Viktor whispers into Henryk's ear.

"We're celebrating the ghetto's productivity. Things are looking up, Viktor. You'll see. Just listen."

"But what about the traveler and the gas vans?"

"I personally spoke to the president. There's no truth to any of it."

"How can you be so sure?"

"Enough, Viktor. Today is about celebrating our efforts."

"*Efforts?*"

"Be happy."

As other ghetto councilors and prominent community members take their seats at the long table, Viktor gets up to walk around the exhibition of intricately embroidered bedding and colorful brassieres, expertly-sewn undergarments and delicate lingerie, all of it destined for Nazi Germany and even, according to one vendor, Paris and Rome.

Reality ceases to make sense when Viktor returns to his seat at the long banquet table. "What's happening to us, Henryk?"

Henryk ignores the question. "Viktor, there are rumors of a symphony happening in the ghetto. It's a sign."

"What are you talking about?"

"At the ghetto's House of Culture! They're going to be renovating it this summer. Rumkowski is going to start putting on symphonies in the ghetto—the rescue through work policy is working, Viktor! It's finally happening. The deportations *are* slowing! Don't you see, Viktor? Why would they even consider a symphony at the House of Culture if they really wanted us gone?"

"And when is this symphony happening?"

"We don't know yet. August. Maybe September. We're going to get through this, Viktor. You must have faith."

The room falls silent at President Rumkowski's arrival. First, he acknowledges the uncomfortable reality of celebrating the ghetto's productivity in the looming shadow of deportations, but he promises the rest of the ghetto will be safe, for the "resettlement" will only affect some twenty-thousand "degenerates"—lunatics and inmates, gypsies and thieves, sex workers and criminals to be deported alongside their families.

~~President Rumkowski actually said this~~ Viktor can hardly believe his ears: "It is a most uncompromising order, but one I had to carry out so as to prevent others from doing it. Now, when I am deporting all kinds of connivers and cheats, I do it fully convinced that they asked for this fate. I have assigned for deportation that element of our ghetto which was a festering boil … this commission guarantees, basically, that it will designate people for deportation only if they deserve it."

A council member sitting across from Viktor stands up and leaves. Viktor stays seated. "Morality" is nothing more than the sharpest tool of the oppressor, which is why after the exhibition's reception, Viktor steals as much bread, potatoes, and dried meat as he can to bring home to the starving Czech family downstairs.

Viktor knocks at their door but nobody comes. Upstairs, Martin is vomiting in the kitchen sink again.

"It's nothing, just a bad potato," Martin coughs into a handkerchief speckled with blood.

"How was your day?" Martin asks. "Did your contact say anything about a new work permit?"

Viktor is lightheaded. "Don't worry. The permit is coming," he lies and sticks his head out the window to avoid further questions. According to the new labor regulations, Martin is now too old to work in the ghetto factories, and it's only thanks to a previously forged work permit that he hasn't been deported yet. But Viktor already owes too many favors to his contact in the Department of Labor. He looks out towards the moonlight, where somewhere beyond the firebreak—but how is this possible?—he hears an elephant's trumpet. *I must be hallucinating.*

Martin stands at Viktor's side. "Would you mind if I slept in the bed tonight? I pulled my back this afternoon at the workshop. The foreman has it out for me. If there's another inspection, I'm done for."

"Of course, friend, take the bed. And don't worry, we'll find another permit. I promise. Would you like some tea before sleep?"

"No, thank you. Not tonight," Martin lowers his body into Viktor's bed.

"I'll get the fire going. Have an extra blanket."

"Good night, friend," Martin turns his body to face the wall.

Viktor peers up at his mostly-empty bookshelf and stands on his tiptoes to pull down yet another book for kindling. He hoped he wouldn't have to burn this one, a 1900 first edition of *The Wonderful Wizard of Oz* by Frank L. Baum, a gift from Helen. She gave it to him in London when they first started dating, to help with his English. Viktor goes to the kitchen and turns on the potbelly stove and reads the first sentence before unceremoniously ripping out the first pages and tossing them into the fire: "Folklore, legends, myths and fairy tales have followed childhood through the ages, for every healthy youngster has a wholesome and instinctive love for stories fantastic, marvelous and manifestly unreal."

After finishing the last of his Earl Grey tea, bartered with a council member for a luxury Montegrappa fountain pen, Viktor eases himself onto the floor and tries to get comfortable. His stiff, withering body is numb from exhaustion, but his mind is once again kept awake by the numbers: 10,003 deportees in January, 7,025 in February, and 24,687 in March. *How can this be?* Viktor thinks about the Polish family of five that was chosen because their sons were petty thieves, and he remembers the elderly

Luxembourgian couple and their grandchild—what were their names?—who asked him so politely at registration if anything could be done. He thinks of the German family from Münster whose son was a well-known soccer player before the war, can still hear their horrified confusion when Viktor told them their son's celebrity wouldn't save him. Viktor no longer pretends that closing his eyes will help him sleep. Tomorrow will be more of the same, another day of impossible questions, and the fire will still crackle in the potbelly stove, its mouth bathed in an orange glow.

Viktor throws off his itchy woolen blankets and stands at the bookshelf again, craning his neck to look up at his dwindling collection. He pulls down Alfred Adler's *The Science of Living* and, as he reads a dog-eared page, has a memory of attending one of Professor Adler's lectures in Vienna. "No human being can think, feel, will, dream without being determined, continued, modified and directed, towards an ever-present objective." Viktor tosses the entire book into the fire and watches it consume Adler's wisdom. The list in his ledger grows:

254. *The Wonderful Wizard of Oz*

255. *The Science of Living*

As he stares at the popping embers, Viktor is visited by a hazy memory of Elsa Dietrich. That was almost three years ago. *What did she look like? How did she smell? What was the precise color of her red dress?* Viktor closes his eyes in search of illumination, but he doesn't care to live in a world in which she only exists in memory. Tonight, more than anything, Viktor hopes he can finally forget her.

Today is a portent, Witches' Night, April 30, 1942. It's been exactly two years since the ghetto was sealed. Elsa has endured life as Carl's reluctant mistress and Major Brandt's caretaker with the daily abuse of opiates, amphetamines, and copious amounts of wine. Her current arrangement with Carl gives her monthly access to a police vehicle, which she uses to visit Rachel and the children and to help other families hiding in the countryside. As for Viktor, Elsa doesn't know what to do. The Łódź Ghetto is the most iso-lated in all of Poland, and Elsa doesn't dare attempt re-en-tering after last year's near-fatal run-in with a ghetto sen-try. Her resistance at the office has long surpassed wads of mucus and amphetamines in Brandt's coffee, however: instead of drugging Major Brandt, whose massive stroke left him a paraplegic, she's now focused on scouring the ghetto registry for easy-to-change birthdays.

The upcoming resettlements are targeting children and the elderly, which is why today, just like yesterday and the day before, Elsa is altering birth years in the registry. She's already changed hundreds of the elders' birth dates from the 1860s to the 1880s (by transforming the 6s into 8s, eighty-year-olds magically return to their sixties) with-out ignoring the terrible truth that for every elder she saves with a clerical error, thousands of others will still be con-demned. Still, it feels better than nothing. What else can she do within the machinery of destruction but try and save as many people as she can?

Major Brandt's massive stroke didn't just paralyze the muscles on the left side of his body—it also turned him into a more subdued man. Bound to a wheelchair and no longer able to descend into the cellar, Brandt can no longer write correctly with his atrophied muscles, thus relying on Elsa to transcribe his rants. Brandt spends his days holed up in his office, drinking tea as he pours over pseudoscientific texts from esteemed "racial scientists" in Berlin. Today, he's listening to blues and jazz records in hopes of pinpointing the characteristics of "degenerate witchcraft music."

"It's incredible, really. It's all going according to plan ..." Brandt slurs over the scratching voice of Robert Johnson. He hands Elsa an expense report from the *Kulmhof* labor camp detailing 32,429.35 Reichsmarks spent for twelve one-way transports from *Litzmannstadt*.

The spectral voice of Robert Johnson singing "Come On In My Kitchen" sends a chill down Elsa's spine as she looks over the numbers: a dozen outbound trains carrying a total of 10,993 travelers at RM 2.95 per traveler and an invoice for just thirteen return tickets to *Litzmannstadt*.

Oh, she's gone, I know she won't come back

I've taken the last nickel out of her nation sack

You better come on in my kitchen

It's goin' to be rainin' outdoors

"It moves you, doesn't it?" Brandt raises his mug of tea with his better hand. "It moves me too. And it's precisely because it moves us that this degenerate music is so dangerous."

Elsa feigns agreement and puts down the expense report. The haunting song is relentless.

Oh, can't you hear that wind howl?

Oh, can't you hear that wind howl?

You better come on in my kitchen

Well, it's goin' to be rainin' outdoors

Half of Brandt's paralyzed face smiles with genuine

joy; the other side struggles to break free of its grimace. "Music has the power to teach us everything we need to know about a people. It can instill fear just as well as it can inspire hope—and delusion. We will soon begin permitting the Jews to put on symphonies at the ghetto's House of Culture. Needless to say, after this summer, they will need it …"

Elsa doesn't take the bait. She knows exactly what he means.

"It will be fascinating to see how they react," Brandt continues. "At the end of summer, their symphony will perform Beethoven's Fifth and Schubert's *Erlkönig*. It promises to be a fascinating spectacle, Elsa, to which I have arranged for special passes into the ghetto to witness. But there is still much work to be done. It's going to be a busy summer, indeed: I have been tasked with sterilizing and renovating over one thousand ghetto buildings. I need disinfectant. Please call the new IG Farben facility and ask about the Zyklon-B chemical. We will use it as a trial run before the buildings are liquidated. My contacts tell me that Zyklon-B is particularly useful for fighting pests and disinfecting ships, trains, and warehouses. In fact, General Governor Hans Frank has made some interesting findings at the camp outside of Lublin. Perhaps you should visit the authorities there."

"And which camp is that exactly?"

"Majdanek."

"Yes, Herr Brandt. I'll call them later today."

"No. Take the car now. Best not to discuss these things over the phone."

Smoke rises in the countryside, out on the horizon,

from the pyres set ablaze for *Walpurgisnacht*. It used to be Elsa's favorite childhood holiday, a festival commemorating the beginning of spring, or the end of winter. She always celebrated Walpurgis Night with her father in the Harz Forest, where in the German tradition, on April 30 atop the Brocken, the highest peak in the Harz Mountains, the region's many witches, demons, and ghouls gather to revel with the Devil.

At least, this is the version of the story Elsa was taught to remember. Saint Walpurga was a heroic Christian missionary who warded off evil spirits and fought dark magic throughout Germany, and every year on the morning of April 30, Elsa would wait at the edge of the forest until her father said the evil spirits had left, so she could search for small gifts hidden amongst the trees. Elsa loved the excitement of the tradition in spite of the lingering fear that she'd spend her summers playing in a forest where demons had been.

An hour into the drive towards the camp outside of Lublin, Elsa comes across a young couple walking along the side of the road, dragging two large suitcases behind them.

Elsa rolls down the window. "Would you like a ride?" She says in Polish.

"No, thank you." The boy grips his lover's hand tightly.

Elsa knows what they're fleeing. "I can get you to the Vistula."

The teenage girl whispers something into her lover's ear, but he pulls her away and continues down the road.

Elsa rolls alongside them and pleads with the boy to reconsider. "I'm here to help. It's not safe to be walking here with all of the local patrols. You must get off the road."

The girl pulls the boy backward and studies Elsa with tearful eyes. She whispers again into the boy's ear and hugs him; the boy concedes with a petulant, "Fine!"

Elsa helps them load their suitcases into the trunk. Over the past year and a half, she's helped dozens of mostly young people reach the sandy banks of the Vistula River, but today is the first time she's met people fleeing south.

"Be careful," Elsa warns. "There's a huge camp outside of Lublin. Where are you headed?"

"Oświęcim," the girl says.

Elsa recognizes the name from a recent bill from a newly operational IG Farben factory outside of a town called Oświęcim.

"Is that where you're from?" Elsa tries to catch the boy's eyes in the rear-view mirror, but he stares out the window instead.

"We come from Radom, but we had to leave," the girl says. "The killings are starting again."

"Avoid Oświęcim. It isn't safe there."

"What do you know about what is safe?" The boy snaps.

"We have someone who can hide us there," the girl says.

"Dark rumors are coming from the camp in that town," Elsa warns. "Please, go further south along the river. Stay away from the roads."

The teenage boy snaps at her again. "What do you know about rumors? The whole world is a rumor. Why should we trust a German anyway?"

Elsa remains silent until they reach the river. She drops off the young couple in a dense cluster of aquatic trees where a man in a rowboat is waiting.

"You're Moishe's friends, are you?" The man wades towards them through the river grass. "You're early."

The teenagers lift their suitcases above their heads and pile them into the boat.

Elsa watches from the sand. "At least wait until dark to pass Puławy. There are troops stationed there."

"This isn't my first time," the boatman croaks. "You're the Nazi secretary, aren't you? I've heard about you. I thought you were a ghost."

The boy curses at Elsa and spits at her feet. "Come on," he grabs the girl's hand, but she resists.

"Don't go near Oświęcim," Elsa gives the girl a bar of chocolate and places a wad of złoty in her hand. "Keep going south until you reach the Carpathians."

"We don't take advice from Germans," the boy yanks his partner deeper into the shallows, climbs into the boat, and pushes off the shore.

The rest of the drive to the Majdanek camp is uneventful. When she arrives, however, the guards tell her to turn around. Despite Elsa's credentials, the unbending camp guards insist she cannot enter today. Elsa eyes the camp's billowing smokestacks in the rearview mirror and continues to Rachel and the children in Wymagamówka, where her black sedan comes to a halt next to the barn.

Wladyslaw greets and thanks her for the picnic basket filled with eggs, meat, bread, and cheese, reassures Elsa that Rachel's mother-in-law is *still* senile and delirious and that none of the villagers have asked any more questions after the children were caught playing in a neighbor's field.

Wladyslaw escorts Elsa up a rickety wooden ladder to

reach Rachel and the children in the barn.

"Happy Witches night, my little ones," she pats Ania and Little Tadeusz on the head. Ania is wearing a white, cone-shaped paper hat that fits loosely. Little Tadeusz straddles his wooden hobbyhorse, a recent birthday gift from Elsa.

He prances back and forth along the hayloft. "I'll get you witches!"

"Quiet, my child," Rachel scoops him in her arms. "Wladyslaw? Can you take the children down into the barn? Me and Elsa need to speak."

"Can we jump?" Little Tadeusz asks.

"Pleeeease!" Ania says.

"Okay, but it's only because Aunt Elsa is here."

Elsa and Rachel lift each child by the armpits and drop them down onto a pile of hay.

"The *Luftwaffe* has been pushed back in Britain," Elsa informs Rachel. "The battle continues in the east. The Russians have mounted a counter-offensive."

"What about Viktor?"

"As far as I know, he's still working for the council's Department of Statistics. The authorities say an epidemic of spotted fever has broken out ..."

Rachel shakes her head. "The ghetto won't last another year. What about the British and the Americans? "

"They say the Americans are planning an amphibious assault from North Africa. The British control the skies over London, and there's talk of a British raid along the French coast. Still, it's hard to know what's true ..."

"And what about the camp outside of Lublin?"

Elsa remains silent for a time. She doesn't have the words to describe it. "Majdanek. I tried to visit today, but there was a roadblock."

"So the rumors are true …"

"They're not using gas vans anymore. It's something much bigger."

Rachel stares wide-eyed at the children playing down below. Their laughter swirls up into the hayloft. "But how is it possible?"

Elsa reveals all she knows. "I've seen the train reports from all over the region. The outbound ones carry thousands of people but return empty. Trainloads of clothing, shoes, and unopened suitcases stacked to the ceilings in Pabianice …"

"So it's true then. They're exterminating us."

Elsa's voice falters. "I don't know what happens in the camps. All I know is nobody sent there comes back."

"How can you not know what's happening?"

"I can't be certain if … Major Brandt won't admit to anything. He barely speaks of anything since his trip to Wannsee in January."

"Come play with us!" Little Tadeusz calls up to Rachel and Elsa. She squeezes Rachel's hand and looks her in the eyes. "I promise I'll find out."

"Come here, children," Elsa climbs down the ladder and crouches on one knee. "Tonight is Witches' Night. Do you know what that means?"

"That we have to kill them!" Little Tadeusz says.

"Not kill, Tadeusz. Scare them away. Witches' Night— it's called *Hexennacht* in German. Can you say *Hexennacht*?

It's the final battle between winter and spring, the night when all the ghosts and evil spirits come out to play. But there are good ones, too, Tadeusz, and with the Powerful Princess Ania and you, the Brave Knight, protecting your Queen, the evil spirits stand no chance."

"So we have to fight the monsters?" Ania asks. Her cone-shaped hat slips over her eyes.

Wladyslaw smiles and adjusts her hat. "Yes, we do have to fight the monsters. We will light a candle this evening and put it in the window, okay? The light will scare away the bad spirits and serve as a beacon for the good ones. The demons are afraid of the warmth of the flames."

"Are they close?" Little Tadeusz wonders.

"No," Elsa replies. "They're far, far away, gathering in the Harz Mountains."

Little Tadeusz is confused. "Where are the Heart Mountains?"

Elsa smiles and ruffles the boy's hair. "The Heart Mountains. I like that. The Heart Mountains are where I come from, in Northern Germany."

"Isn't that where the Skeleton Men come from, too?"

"Yes, that's right," Elsa swallows hard. "The Skeleton Men do come from there. And tonight, the wicked are gathering for a final festival before the summer scares them away for good."

"Why are they wicked?" Ania asks.

"Maybe they're just scared," Little Tadeusz says. "That's why they're hiding in the Heart Mountains?"

"Yes. Precisely, my child," Wladyslaw replies. "The Skeleton Men are afraid."

Elsa turns to hide her tears from the children. She gathers herself and smiles. "Ah! Children! I almost forgot the most important thing: the secret weapon!" She fetches her handbag and pulls out two bars of chocolate.

"Not yet, my little ones. It's very important to stay quiet and be patient. You must wait until nightfall to eat the chocolate, okay? And you must remember to listen to your mother and do whatever she says. Can you promise me that, children?"

Little Tadeusz and Ania shake their heads with purpose as they fixate on the chocolate.

Elsa hugs both of them tightly. "You mustn't go outside unless your mother tells you. Don't let the wicked spirits into the barn, okay?"

"Or the Skeleton Men either!" Ania squeaks.

"Yes, my sweet Ania. Or the Skeleton Men. If you light the spirit candle and obey your mother and Wladyslaw, you'll be protected while I'm away. I promise. I'll be back very soon."

"Where are you going?" Little Tadeusz pulls at Elsa's coat.

"I need to warn the other children about the witches. And next time, if the good spirits have prevailed, I'll be back with a very special friend. Wouldn't you like that?"

The children jump up and down in unison. Elsa kisses each on the forehead and walks out to the car with Rachel.

"You really think you can find Viktor?" Rachel asks.

"I'll get the opportunity to enter the ghetto this summer. They're putting on a symphony at the House of Culture. Brandt wants me to attend."

"A symphony?" Rachel snaps in exasperation. "Are you serious? So you don't have a plan? You're just assuming you'll waltz into the ghetto and bump into Viktor and save him?"

Elsa looks away. "I'm still working on it ..."

Rachel furrows her brow. "There's not enough time … do you know who's living in our old apartment?"

"They keep it for long-term visitors, usually Nazi bureaucrats and dignitaries."

"Do you know if the wardrobe is still there?"

"I don't see why it wouldn't be."

Rachel's eyes light up. "Check. The wardrobe has a secret compartment in the back. Tadeusz built it himself. Viktor knows about it. Find the wardrobe and have it sent to the Ghetto Workshops Bureau for some basic repair ... the foreman, Singer, was Tadeusz's friend. If he's still alive, he'll help us."

Some four hundred kilometers away, Carl wakes from a recurring nightmare of a black silverfish burrowing into his belly button and swimming through his intestines, using its many legs to skitter up his esophagus and screech out of his mouth.

Carl hugs his pillow to his chest. His sheets are damp with sour sweat. He looks at the unfinished letter to Elsa on his bedside table and considers calling again. *Elsa, I miss you. I want to get back to us again. I sleep so much better next to you, darling. I keep having this dream. My time with you last year feels so far away.*

The violet morning sky illuminates the crowded

barracks. Carl climbs down from his top bunk and takes a swig of vodka. Today will be more of the same: the screech of a train whistle, a guttural chugging in the distance before the rolling clouds of smoke and silver steam consume the train station. The pistons will hiss and spit like always as the iron behemoth groans to a halt on the platform. But the year is 1942, and these trains are no longer bringing life into the city—they are extracting it—so once again, Carl will lose himself in canteens full of vodka and tubes of Pervitin to confront this terror, days of frenzy herding thousands of human beings into cattle cars destined "for the East."

Carl's day begins at the ghetto's Central Prison, where a group of Hungarian refugees branded as criminals has been confined to a barbed-wire enclosure with nothing but cold hard earth and scraps of bread. They plead and ask Carl questions in a language he doesn't understand. Overwhelmed, Carl takes a cigarette break and speaks to a young reservist who reminds him of a childhood friend. Hours later, Carl escorts the Hungarians to the train station, shoving the men into the walls and threatening the women with the butt of his rifle.

"Stop crying! You're being resettled!" He's tired of explaining. "There'll be more food in the East. It's even warmer, too. Don't believe the rumors; there's no truth to them."

Carl wants to believe his words still matter. He wants to believe he still has a chance of happiness with Elsa, even as he brutalizes a group of teenagers into a waiting train wagon. He wants to believe in a world in which Elsa doesn't recoil from his touch, a world in which vodka and Pervitin are not his lords, a world in which all of this will soon be over, and everything will be okay.

On the train platform, three emaciated teenagers tell the deportees to sell everything they have. "Only food and money will do you any good!" One says. "How much for that scarf? And what about that watch?" Many of the deportees begin catching on, trying to sell what they can for food and petty cash before the German police use their nightsticks to break up the impromptu market. Carl and the other police officers line up shoulder to shoulder and begin to move in on the huddled masses. He uses his rifle to corral families together, yelling at them to stay calm, keep quiet, and get on the trains quickly. Some soil themselves in terror—the smell nauseates him in the rising heat—but he does his best to avoid eye contact, especially with the mothers, his eyes focused on what's above, pushing forward arm-in-arm with the other policemen.

When it's finally over and the cattle cars are filled with terrified people, ghetto policemen arrive to gather the suitcases and rucksacks and pillows and blankets left behind. Some put dolls and wooden hobby horses and clay sculptures and rubber balls into wheelbarrows, while others collect pots and pans and silverware and hair clips, unbroken perfume bottles and elegant fountain pens, decks of playing cards and dominoes sets, rings, necklaces and bracelets, anything deemed valuable or otherwise worth bartering. Carl watches the same young reservist from earlier pick up a child's stuffed animal and hide it in his jacket. He decides to follow him to the Office of Resettled Persons, where the names of the deportees are transformed into a statistic and sorted into a filing cabinet at the German Ghetto Administration.

To celebrate the end of the latest round of deportations,

hundreds of battalion men, soldiers, and SS officers relocate to a jam-packed bar. Carl finishes his vodka and orders another, chasing it down with dark ale to drown out the day. Someone jostles Carl from behind and splatters beer on his shoulder. He reacts instinctively, spinning around to punch the offender, but the bar is too crowded for him to raise his fist, and the sea of drunken soldiers is rising and crashing all around him, showering him with beer as it hoists fresh pints into the air.

The mass chants an impromptu song in the name of a deranged victory:

Bye-bye, Jew, so long, farewell
The Bolsheviks will welcome you to the gates of hell!

The horde of men crushes Carl's torso into the sharp edge of the bar. He loosens his collar and takes shallow breaths. The imagined black insect is back again—he can feel it in his belly, the unreal silverfish gnashing at his intestines, cleaning its glossy black mouthparts, antennae twitching in search of escape.

"Are you okay?"

Carl turns to see the young reservist from the Office of Resettled Persons. The teenager puts his hand on Carl's shoulder and places the stuffed toy of a black dog in front of him.

Suddenly, the crowd starts to dissipate.

"Another vodka, please," Carl orders. "Do you want one?"

"The major says we should get some rest," the reservist says. "We're moving out tomorrow to a town called Bilgoraj."

"What's there?" Carl asks, but he's only half listening,

is staring into the beady black eyes of the stuffed toy dog.

"They say it's a special assignment."

"Anything but the trains," Carl says.

"I agree."

"Who's the toy for?"

"My future son."

"You have a woman?"

"I love a woman."

"What's the difference?"

"She didn't want me to come here."

"So why did you?"

"Duty, I guess. Or maybe I was scared."

"Scared of what?"

"Isn't it obvious?"

"Nothing seems obvious anymore."

"You should get some rest, Carl."

"I haven't had a good night's sleep in months. Longer, probably. How do you know my name?"

"We have to be up early. It's time to go. You should drink some water."

"Don't tell me what to do, boy. Bartender, another vodka, please. Get this greenhorn out of my sight."

The reservist abides and the sharp pain returns to Carl's abdomen. He slips his hand beneath his undershirt and grabs at his stomach, stumbles when he stands up, holds onto the bar for balance and rushes out of the bar to vomit in the street, but he can still feel the silverfish scratching at his intestines.

Three years since the sirens began, and Viktor's life in the Łódź Ghetto is coming to an end. He no longer remembers what life was like before, when he could still order a coffee on a terrace and walk to the other side of town. The past has become a dream, the present a nightmare, the future an illusion. All that matters now is keeping his body alive, because after Rumkowski's speech earlier today, a healthy body is the only hope left.

From his window, Viktor watches the horrors transpiring down below. As soon as Rumkowski's speech ended, Ghetto police swarmed the streets to inform the terrified families of what was to come. German transport trucks pulled up in front of hospitals and began collecting the young and the elderly; those who couldn't descend the stairs were thrown out of windows or simply shot in their beds.

"We have to find somewhere to hide you," Viktor tells Martin, who's reading *Civilization and Its Discontents* from the comfort of Viktor's bed. "It's happening again. They want twenty-thousand more. A work pass won't save you this time, Martin."

Viktor watches two more German troop transports roll towards the medical facility on Mickiewicza Street with a squad of ghetto police in tow. "Incredible, really. Three years to the day since I sat at this very window and watched this all begin."

"What exactly did Rumkowski say in his speech?" Martin coughs violently.

"They're coming for all children under ten, the sick, and the elderly. Twenty-thousand more. I saw Calel but he didn't look me in the eye. He knows you're here, Martin. You have to hide."

"Where am I going to go, Viktor?" Martin flips through a few more pages of *Civilization and Its Discontents*. "If they come for me, they can take me. I won't have someone else go in my place."

"Now you're being the idiot." Viktor knew this day would come, but he didn't expect President Rumkowski's speech to be so eloquently devastating. From the moment Rumkowski took the stage, he gripped the podium with shaking hands. The president's hair was much grayer and thinner than when Viktor first met him, and he no longer resembled anything close to "King Chaim."

The air was hot and thick with trepidation as Rumkowski cleared his throat. ~~President Rumkowski actually said this:~~ "The ghetto has been struck a hard blow. They demand what is most dear to it—children and the elderly. I was not privileged to have a child of my own and, therefore, devoted my best years to children. I lived and breathed together with children. I never imagined that my own hands would be forced to make this sacrifice on the altar. In my old age, I am forced to stretch out my hands and beg: 'Brothers and sisters, give them to me! Fathers and mothers, give me your children …'"

Terrible wails swept through the crowd as ghetto police tried to quell the frantic questions: "How old?" "How young?" "Where will they go?"

Rumkowski held out his hands in supplication. "Yesterday, I was given the order to send away more than twenty thousand Jews from the ghetto, and if I did not? 'We will do it ourselves,' the question arose: should we have accepted this and carried it out ourselves, or left it to others? I must carry out this difficult and bloody operation. I must cut off the limbs in order to save the body!"

"Cut off the limbs to save the body," Martin laughs. "Just like a surgeon. So what does that make me? An infected big toe?"

In the square, the idea had been too horrific for many to bear. Some women fainted where they stood, crushed between the masses, brought back to consciousness with a slap to the face; others threw what few objects they still owned at the podium; more than a few men came to blows after colliding into each other in an attempt to escape the crowd and return to their families before it was too late.

"Did he actually say *give us your children?*" Martin puts down his book.

"He tried reassuring the crowd that at least he'd saved all the children over ten. And then he said there were hospital patients who could only expect to live a few more days. *Give me the sick so we can save the healthy*, he said."

Martin chuckles. "Give us your babies and your wrinkled elders and all who sneeze! My God. What a world. How did he end it?"

"He said if we deliver the twenty thousand ourselves, there wouldn't be any more deportations. *It takes the heart of a thief to demand what I'm demanding of you*, he said. He asked us to put ourselves in his position, think logically, and come to our own conclusions."

"Well. At least his logic is sound. I'd do the same. Wouldn't you? If the survival strategy is rescue through work, logic demands only the healthy should be kept alive. I guess that's curtains for me."

"Everything's upside down."

"Not upside down, Viktor. Exactly what is to be

expected. Hey, listen to this," Martin reads a final passage from *Civilization and Its Discontents*: "'The fateful question for the human species seems to me to be whether and to what extent their cultural development will succeed in mastering the disturbance of their communal life by the human instinct of aggression and self-destruction.'"

Viktor moves from the window to sit next to Martin in the bed. He props himself up against the wall with a pillow pressed into the small of his back. "Would you read me the rest of it? It's my favorite of all book endings."

Martin sits up, taps Viktor's knee with the spine of the book and clears his throat: "'Men have gained control over the forces of nature to such an extent that with their help they would have no difficulty in exterminating one another to the last man. They know this, and hence comes a large part of their current unrest, their unhappiness and their mood of anxiety. And now it is to be expected that the other of the two 'Heavenly Powers,' eternal Eros, will make an effort to assert himself in the struggle with his equally immortal adversary. But who can foresee with what success and with what result?'"

A dog whistle blares and now the marching of boots in unison.

"It would appear that Freud was right," Martin says. "Thanatos has finally come to take stock of the situation, old friend."

Viktor squeezes Martin's hand and looks him in the eye. There's no other way to say it. "It's been a pleasure living with you, Martin. I love you, my friend."

"And it will be an honor to die with you!" Martin squeezes Viktor's hand as a torrent of footsteps rumbles up the stairwell and crashes at the apartment threshold with a loud banging.

There's no mistaking Calel's voice on the other side of the door. "Viktor! Martin! I know you're in there! Open up! Open the door now!"

"He's not taking me alive," Martin squeezes Viktor's shoulder and walks to the kitchen, where he turns on the overhead light and places a glass vial of cyanide on the table.

"I've been saving it since they got here," Martin says. "Want one? My treat."

Viktor hisses at him. "Not yet. We're lucky it's just Calel. Just wait."

"The Gestapo could be standing right behind him," Martin retorts and pours two healthy glasses of vodka.

"Are you alone, Calel?" Viktor speaks into the door.

"Yes! Open up! Right. Now!"

"Do you swear it?"

"Yes!"

Viktor cracks the door.

"Tell me where they are, you fool!" Calel barrels across the threshold, grabbing Viktor by the collar and shoving him into the nearly empty bookshelf. Calel's face is swollen and red—he's put on weight since Viktor last saw him—and it only turns more crimson as Calel tries to squeeze the words out of Viktor.

"Tell me where they are! I won't ask again!" Calel raises his truncheon.

"You coward! You snake! Get your filthy hands off him!" Martin attacks Calel from behind and manages to wrench the truncheon from Calel's grasp and throw it to the floor, but Martin's feat of strength comes at the expense of his lungs. He falls to one knee and wheezes violently.

"The Czech family," Calel comes at Viktor again, pointing his index finger like a weapon. "They aren't downstairs. So where are they? They've already skipped two registrations. Where are you hiding them?"

"Calel, I swear I don't know—"

"Don't bullshit me, Viktor! You have to respect me!" Calel shoves Viktor back up against the bookshelf. "I know you spoke to them after Rumkowski's speech! You've been feeding them stolen food from the council. Where are they, Viktor? I won't ask again."

"Would you look at that!" Martin regains his composure and puts himself in between Calel and Viktor. "Now you fancy yourself a thug, is it? We don't know anything about the family downstairs, and we wouldn't tell you if we did, you rat."

Calel lunges for the truncheon on the ground, but Viktor beats him to it.

"Calel, please, let's just all calm down," Viktor throws the truncheon across the room and places his hand on Calel's shoulder. "What are we doing? Come on, let's go to the kitchen and have some vodka."

"I'm not drinking with him," Martin spits at Calel's feet.

"Just one drink," Viktor says. "For old time's sake."

Calel and Martin refuse to look at each other at the small kitchen table. Viktor pours a third glass.

"So, you'll drink the council's liquor but won't help me save my family?" Calel says. "I should have you arrested.

You're going to get me killed."

Martin laughs. "Getting a head-start on tomorrow's quota, are you, boy? The man served you a glass. Drink it."

"Martin, please," Viktor raises his glass. "Stop it. Both of you. You're acting like children. Let's enjoy this drink. Remember we used to be friends."

Martin's glare softens with each sip, as does Calel's clenched jaw, and his puffed-out chest deflates once his glass is empty.

After a second vodka, Calel begins to weep. "You don't understand. I didn't want to come here tonight, but what else can I do? I was supposed to deliver the Czech family yesterday—their children are on the list, Viktor, and I have a quota to meet. If I don't deliver them … Viktor, they're going to take my wife and daughter. You have to help."

"He doesn't have to do anything," Martin says.

Viktor is too tired to lie. "Calel, I don't know where they are, truly, but it wouldn't matter if I did."

"How can you say that?" Calel's anger is mounting again. "Why are you protecting them? The Dutch family downstairs said they *saw you speaking to them* this morning!"

"They're lying to save their own children," Viktor explains.

Martin interjects. "Do you really think Viktor would condemn four children and six adults just to save you?"

"Yes, Martin, actually, I do," Calel stands up. "Viktor works at the Department of Statistics, after all. He condemns hundreds of children every day!"

Viktor's face grows hot. Calel isn't wrong.

"So it's either us or them, is it?" Martin finishes his

second glass.

"I have to fill my quota for this resettlement," Calel says.

"*Resettlement*. Call it what it is, boy: they're exterminating us. *That's* why you've come here tonight, Calel."

"No. We don't know where they're sending us. Truly, I don't know. Some have sent postcards from the camp near Koło. They say it's not that bad."

"Postcards!" Martin laughs. "You think we're going to rat out an entire family and put them on a train because of a few miraculous postcards?"

Calel lowers his head and hides his face in his hands. "They'll put my daughter on the train if I don't fill my quota," he trembles. "She's only nine years old, Viktor. I won't let her go alone. I have to give them something …"

"You mean *someone*," Martin corrects him.

Calel's body sinks deeper into his chair. He looks like his old self again—unsure, naïve, unprepared—almost innocent.

Calel stares into Viktor's eyes. "Viktor, please. Another day, another hour … it's all I have left. You must tell me where the Czech family is … I have no other choice."

"There's always a choice," Martin replies.

"And I've made mine, Calel," Viktor answers. "Martin is right: we don't know where they are, truly, and I wouldn't tell you if I did. I did see them this morning, but when I returned from Rumkowski's speech, they weren't there."

Calel stares at Viktor with bloodshot eyes. His broken demeanor mutates into an unnatural show of strength. This time, when he stands up, he widens his stance, puffs out his chest, and lifts his fist. Only now does Viktor notice just how bruised and swollen Calel's knuckles are.

"You fools," Calel wipes away his tears. "You condemn thousands at the council and you house this decrepit faggot at your own risk. You'll be the death of him, Martin, mark my words."

Martin pulls out his glass vial of cyanide and shakes it in Calel's face. "Nobody here is afraid of you, boy ... or of death, either. You've been a terrified child since the beginning."

"And you've become an old man," Calel retorts. "Give me a name. One name, Viktor. You should know better than anyone else how this works."

Viktor shakes his head. "I give you nothing, Calel. I've already given more than I can bear."

Martin produces two cigarettes from his chest pocket and hands one to Viktor. "Get out of here, Calel. We won't be led like sheep to the slaughter. There's nothing left to say. You might be too young to have principles, but a guilty conscience lasts a lifetime."

"You're wrong. I might have blood on my hands, but history will forgive me ..."

Martin takes a long drag from his cigarette. "History forgives nothing. It only ever forgets."

Calel straightens his back. "Very well. So long, Viktor." He taps his feet together like a military man and slams the door.

"I always said Calel would be a liability," Martin concludes. "He was never able to possess himself as he is. How pathetic."

"You're wrong, Martin. He has a family. What else

should he do? Maybe he's right—maybe the only dignity left is survival."

"Surviving isn't the same thing as living."

"Well, there's only survival in the ghetto."

"We should go down swinging—I'll go down swinging."

"I'm tired of this war, Martin. I don't want to live like a rodent. We're more than eating, breathing, sleeping, shitting creatures. You're right: survival isn't dignity, but there is dignity in deciding how we go. Will you come with me to the ghetto symphony tomorrow night?"

"On the eve of another deportation? It's obscene, Viktor. Rumkowski and his minions will be there."

"Beethoven will be there, too, Martin. And Schubert."

Martin laughs and raises a final glass. "To your intolerable optimism."

They finish the bottle and Martin soon falls asleep on the floor. Viktor sits on the edge of his bed and relishes listening to Martin's snoring, his lungs expanding and contracting until the wave-like rhythm sends Viktor into his own peaceful reflection.

In some way he feels relief—relief that this is the end. There is comfort here, isn't there, in the certainty of his future? Viktor decides that tomorrow will be his last day at the *Judenrat*. He will celebrate his departure with a night at the symphony. No more rumors, no more questions, no more waiting, no more trains, no more doubts, no more illusions about what's to come.

The light of a waning crescent moon floods into the apartment. A silver sliver. A bitten fingernail. Viktor listens to the world's silence from his window. He imagines a different kind of place somewhere far beyond the ghetto wall, a place where children play by the lakeside and couples kiss in the park, a place where terraces buzz with conversations that spill out into the streets. Viktor imagines a world where a professor is handing out syllabi to a room of eager students before shifting his focus to the beautiful banality of his apartment: a spider web in the top right corner of the room that he's always left alone for some reason; the writing desk Tadeusz once built for him, its hand-carved features fully visible now that it's no longer covered in papers and stacks of unread books; the brown stains on the warped floorboards courtesy of Mrs. Eberhardt's cabbage stews; and now his eyes settle on his bookshelf. Viktor stands on his tiptoes and pulls the remaining texts down to display on his desk: H.G. Well's *War of the Worlds*, Sigmund Freud's *Civilization and Its Discontents*, Friedrich Nietzsche's *Thus Spoke Zarathustra*, Franz Kafka's *The Metamorphosis*, and two books by Mary Shelley, *Frankenstein* and *The Last Man*.

What has he learned? What has he forgotten? Three years ago, he watched artillery fire light up the night sky and flash violence across the landscape. Tonight, Viktor remembers the sound of those first tanks rolling into the city, the trembling teaspoons on saucers, and all of the faces on the terrace. Calel, clumsy Calel, so ill at ease, young and innocent; and what about Henryk and Martin's never-ending debates about faith—but also their friendship; and now Viktor can see her again clearly, too—Elsa—he can smell her orange blossom perfume and see her head down in her ledger and, *oh! the light red wine shade of her dress.* She is still watching him, somehow—maybe she always will be—and how strangely optimistic he felt on that first day when he met her, when Viktor still believed in possibility.

He sighs watching the searchlights scan the horizon.

He's lucky to have once felt alive, to have been in love, to have understood the meaning of true friendship. Every act becomes sacred as he prepares for sleep. Viktor slides a blanket out from under Martin's toes and drapes it oh-so-carefully atop his friend, then hops from one leg to the other to remove his socks. He unbuttons his shirt and goes to the bathroom to relieve himself. Tonight, he relishes in the groans and creaks of the wooden floorboards as he steps over Martin and crawls into bed.

Sitting on the edge of his mattress, Viktor honors the many rituals that remind him of what it means to feel alive. He stretches his neck and arms and straightens his back, careful not to disturb Martin's sleep when he cracks his knuckles and pulls at each toe with a satisfying pop. Viktor drapes a sheet over his own frail body and relishes the cooler side of the pillow; he smiles because even here in the Łódź Ghetto, on the eve of a great destruction, there is still pleasure to be found. Martin's gentle breathing soothes him, and now Viktor remembers what it used to feel like to sleep in the forest as a child, the simple adventure of it, long before he thought he had to make something of himself, long before people started calling him The Professor. He thinks of a time before the answers consumed the questions, a time when life was love and wonder, when he had the instinctual wisdom of a child.

Viktor looks back at the empty bookshelf and cherishes the silence those books promised, long before he thought it necessary to *study* and *take notes*, a time before he associated knowledge with something that had to be proven or put on display. Viktor recalls literature's promise of *elsewhere*, of somewhere far beyond the ghetto wall … of a peaceful cabin in the Swiss Alps, perhaps, or why not the East coast of the

United States, where two lovers might be sitting on a sun-drenched blanket *right now*, reading a book to each other over a bottle of wine. Yes, there must be *someone* beyond this place who's also enjoying this exact moment with Viktor—*why not?*—perhaps on a beach in southern Italy or northern Spain. Viktor remembers what it felt like to swim in the English Channel, to hear the waves and have warm sand slink between his toes. *Oh, the ocean!* How miraculous that Viktor can visit the coast of Normandy from the confines of his apartment and hear the sound of seagulls cawing. And what about that weekend in Switzerland when Helen was healthy? When Viktor's biggest worry was finding dry kindling in the snow. Viktor remembers the first time he saw the world from the top of a mountain and realized he could conquer his fear of heights with a simple pair of wooden skis. Helen was there. *Oh, beautiful Helen.* Tonight, he chooses to remember her fondly.

Viktor breathes deeply. His smile widens, and his eyes well up. *Forgive yourself, Viktor. Forgive yourself for everything. For being selfish, for being impatient, for not listening, for being wrong, for placing work before love, for cultivating intelligence over feeling, for putting your mind before your heart, for favoring certainty over belief.* He used to read and write without needing to qualify or explain. He used to climb up on bookshelves. Tonight, this is what he chooses to remember.

Viktor rearranges his pillow to support his neck. A reassuring thought visits him: much like total happiness is unattainable, so too is its antithesis, for even here in the ghetto, some *thing* still inspires him to believe in the future of a possibility. And how trivial it all seems now, to be afraid of life and death—to worry—when even tonight, Viktor can close his eyes and experience the ocean and the sound of beach waves and a summer sun reflecting off the shore. Even the thought of counting sheep becomes miraculous, for he can hear sheep bleating in a pasture, can feel the breeze of a coastal wind on the back of his neck.

The reality of these memories is a fortification for what's coming. Will he have another chance at a summer morning with her someday, whoever she might be? The touch of warm skin. Of staying beneath the covers just a *little longer* to make love long after the sun has risen. Breakfast in the afternoon—it's still possible, isn't it? And who is Viktor to say it isn't? Oh, to see London one more time at Christmas. To meet an old friend in Vienna. To fall in love in Paris.

Viktor's body decompresses as his heart lets go of something heavy. He is ready for sleep now. He wonders when he might see her again. Will it be in a dream? At a train station? In a blade of grass or a puddle's reflection? Viktor curls up beneath the sheets, whispers, "Goodnight, my love," and gently kisses the back of his hand as an afterthought.

humanity

"Human beings, unwithheld by shame, for they were unbeheld of their fellows, ventured on deeds of greater wickedness, or gave way more readily to their abject fears. Deeds of heroism also occurred, whose very mention swells the heart and brings tears into the eyes. Such is human nature, that beauty and deformity are often closely linked."

—Mary Shelley, *The Last Man*, 1826

When I first wrote these words, I was hurtling through the Arctic darkness, trapped within the confines of a sleek metallic tube some thirty thousand feet above a land of ice.

When I first wrote these words, I was returning home to decide on the next steps of my mother's treatment. Her memory was fading rapidly, and I was the only one she had left. Before my flight, I spoke to the doctor, who suggested I send her to a nursing home.

"You mean a sanatorium. An asylum," I said.

"It's a specialized long-term care facility."

"I'm not locking my mother away in a nursing home like they did with my grandmother."

"We like to think of it as assisted living. It's a beautiful clinic in the mountains. It just opened last year. They offer cutting-edge experimental treatments in a subsidized program for people like your mother."

"You mean people who can't afford regular care. She isn't a guinea pig, doctor. What are these experimental treatments, exactly?"

"I'm prohibited from disclosing that information until you agree to the conditions, but the early results are promising, I can assure you."

"There has to be a better way."

"Listen," the doctor's tone changed. "I'm going to be blunt with you: given the severity of your mother's situation, your options are limited. I can make a call if you'd like. If she qualifies, she could have a private room and a nurse on call twenty-four hours a day."

"Thank you, doctor. But there has to be a better way."

With what little savings I had, I arranged for a caretaker to come by my mother's apartment twice a week.

My mother responded with a defeatist mentality as she flipped through an old photo album. "You're abandoning me like everyone else. You forced me out of my own home. It was my home. Not yours. What's the point of any of this, anyway?" She threw the album on the ground. "I'm already a ghost to everyone. Nobody cares."

Determined to lift her spirits on the day before my departure, I called the owners of our childhood home to ask if it might be possible to spend an hour or two in the backyard. They said they'd be happy to let us visit but that they'd be on vacation. We could still sit on the back porch and enjoy the yard if we liked.

"Where are we going?" My mother asked.

"It's a surprise."

"I'm too old for surprises."

"Get in."

My mother's demeanor changed the moment we pulled into our old neighborhood. From the car window, she pointed out the streets where I used to ride my bicycle and go trick-or-treating. When I parked the car in the cul-de-sac where I'd spent countless summer days, she got out without my help and led the way up the slight incline of our old driveway.

"This was where you first rode a sled. Do you remember? You rode it from the top of the driveway all the way down. And back there—do you remember your tree house?" She pointed towards the wooded area behind the house. "You used to go there as a boy and read the Narnia series with a flashlight. You were so upset when I told you we didn't have a secret wardrobe."

I walked with my mother around the edge of the house. She peered into the windows, cupping her hands on the window panes, peeking back into the past like a curious child. When we reached the backyard, I hugged her and finally let go of something heavy. It had taken me nearly forty years to recognize how much she reminded me of me.

We took our time exploring the woods where I grew up. Her homemade wind chimes still dangled from low-hanging trees, playing the gentle melodies of my youth. The metallic chimes clanged an ethereal song and the thick wooden ones responded with a calming, hollow tone like gentle waves lapping at the side of a rowboat on the seashore. We craned our necks to admire the tall pines, creaking in the breeze, sprinkling needles to the forest floor. We ventured deeper into the woods towards the rusty chain-link fence that protected the edge of the property, stepping over the remnants of my old tree house where, as a teenager, I'd drink cheap vodka with my friends. Standing amongst the ruins, my mother laughed about the time I'd tried to hide a bottle in the wheel well of a neighbor's truck.

We continued deeper into the woods. Migratory birds heading south for the winter squawked as an early-autumn breeze sifted through the forest. We crunched our way towards the edge of the property, transforming pine needles and brittle leaves into terrestrial stardust. When we finally reached the edge of the property, we came across a felled tree that had crushed a large section of the rusty chain-link fence.

I'd never gone beyond this point in my youth. The closest I ever came was to drag old Christmas trees here and heave them to the other side of the fence.

"Thank you for bringing me here," my mother squeezed my hand tightly. "This forest. These trees. I remember all of it."

She looked back over her shoulder towards our old home. "I can still see you as a child, sitting in that tree house at night. You shined your flashlight into the darkness, out beyond the fence. Do you remember?"

"Yes."

"What do you think? Should we keep going?"

"Yes."

I helped my mother climb over the gap in the chain-link fence and for the first time in our lives, we entered the forest together.

The skin beneath Carl's eyes is raw and sunburned, his face taut like dry leather, and the roads are too bumpy for him to write Elsa about his upcoming mission. It sounds simple enough: round up the *Untermenschen* and partisans hiding in the woods, villages, and farmland outside of Bilgoraj. Carl eats well, drinks heavily, snores in the dark, and he spends most of the morning seeking shelter from an uncharacteristically hot September sun. He seeks refuge in the shade of tall trees and hides his face beneath his steel helmet when the battalion moves out.

The battalion's diesel trucks sputter down dusty roads. Carl moves up to the edge of the truck bed to dangle his feet off the edge and watch the earth speed down below. The roar of the land calms his mind until the convoy takes a pit stop next to a pond, where some men get naked and congregate like animals in the shallow waters. Carl stares at their long testicles and retracted penises dangling between their legs. The men splash in the water like children, laughing as if their rifles and machine guns weren't locked and loaded on the shore.

Carl returns to the edge of the truck bed to sit with his new friend.

"So, kid, remind me of your name again?" He asks the young reservist.

"Thomas."

"Sorry about the other night at the bar. I was drunk. With all these new reservists around here, it's nice to put a name to a face."

Thomas smiles and they sit in silence until the battalion returns.

"It isn't good for you to stay apart from the other men

like this," Cornelius tells Carl. "You want a Pervitin? You look tired."

"It's just the heat. And this damn stomach bug. I can't seem to shake it."

The bumpy journey across the simmering land doesn't help with Carl's nausea. He slides his sweaty palms beneath his undershirt to feel at his belly, closes his eyes, takes deep breaths, and tries to think of anything but vomiting. The convoy stops in yet another small town on the edge of yet another dense forest where mobile killing units have been operating.

Carl finds shade in the long shadow of a crumbling church steeple, but his dehydrated brain cracks like the desiccated earth on which he stumbles.

"Take it easy," Thomas grabs him by the armpits to help him stand in the insectan air.

"Can I have some water?"

"You should've refilled at the pond," Cornelius passes Carl his canteen.

"I need food." He slaps at a mosquito on his neck.

"Stop being a pussy," Cornelius punches Carl in the arm. "I'm going to join the SS patrol. See you back at the trucks in twenty minutes."

Carl sits on the ground and pays no mind to the men talking behind his back like cruel schoolchildren. When he feels steady enough to stand, he follows Thomas down a village side street with his Mauser at waist height, the rifle butt pressed firmly into his belly as he inspects burnt homes and piles of rubble.

"Is anybody in here?" He calls out in German as if there could be any survivors.

"Hello?" He sticks his rifle's muzzle through a broken window and stabs at a suspicious bale of hay with his bayonet.

After clearing the next thatched-roof dwelling, something lurches in his stomach. Carl keels over in agony, leans his rifle against a wall, and puts his hands on his knees to catch his breath.

"It's a ghost town out here," a voice says from behind.

Carl lunges for his rifle and spins around to find Thomas smoking a cigarette.

"You've been following me?"

"Want one?" Thomas ignores the question. "Let's head to the square. There's never anybody out here anyway."

"Never. Not a soul."

Thomas hands Carl a cigarette and leads him deeper into the village. With the sun setting behind them, they share the same elongated shadow. Carl and Thomas soon arrive in a small, dusty square with a stone well. Carl looks down into the depths and pulls up the dry rope attached to a wooden bucket caked in mud.

"Empty. You smell that stench? They probably threw a few bodies down there to poison the water."

"What's with him?" Thomas points across the square at an SS man who's grabbed a black cat by the tail and is swinging the wailing creature round and round his head.

"Don't talk so loudly," Carl watches the SS man fling the black cat high into the blood-red sky as another takes a shot at the screeching animal with a rifle but misses.

The other SS men howl with laughter as the cat crashes to the ground and scurries away.

"Otto just got back from the East," Carl explains. "He isn't the kind of guy you want to mess with."

"So the rumors are true? Is that why Otto's here? For the special mission?"

"I don't know anything about that," Carl stares into the well. "Do you have any water?"

"What does *special mission* mean, exactly?"

"Special mission has only ever meant more patrols. They call it that to keep us guessing. We'll be able to tell by the amount of vodka they serve tonight. If it's anything serious, they'll want us fresh and sober in the morning."

Carl's stomach moans. "Where are you from, Thomas?"

"Danzig."

"No shit," Carl slaps the boy on the back. "I grew up on a farm just outside the city."

"Me too!" Thomas smiles. "I thought I would take over the family business, but the war came."

"You and the rest of the Fatherland. What does your father do?"

"My father is dead."

"I'm sure he would've been proud of you, being here."

"My father was anything but proud—not of me, in any case."

Carl changes the subject. "So, why'd you become a policeman?"

"I didn't. I was forced into it. All I wanted to do was work and live on the family farm."

"Maybe after the war?"

"I think it might be too late."

"If you want my advice, Thomas, get back home as

soon as possible. You don't want to end up like them. Let's head back to the trucks. We only ever find ghosts in these villages anyway."

"Where the hell have you been?" Cornelius asks during the ride back to the barracks. "You didn't drink from the well, did you? What's the brass thinking, giving these green-horns rifles? They're sending us farmers and taxi drivers to do warriors' work. They're too ordinary for what's ahead."

"You don't have any water, do you?"

Carl puts his sweaty palms beneath his shirt again. He swears he can feel the thing squirming around his intestines.

"You don't look right. Have some vodka," Cornelius hands Carl a canteen.

Carl takes a swig. *Déjà-vu.* His vision shakes.

"Are you sure you're ready for tomorrow?" Cornelius pats Carl on the back to help him burp like an infant.

"I just need to eat something," Carl says, but when he closes his eyes, he can see the silverfish with its black antennae frantically searching for something to devour within.

"Where's Thomas?" Carl asks.

Cornelius laughs. "Let's get you back to the barracks."

The trains didn't come today and this feels like enough. Martin went to the Ghetto Workshops Bureau at dawn to speak to the foreman (Singer, one of Tadeusz's old colleagues) about a new work permit, and Viktor promised to save Martin a seat at tonight's symphony in case he's running late. So long as Martin can stay hidden for the next round-up, Viktor is confident Calel will find someone else to put in Martin's stead.

Viktor left the council offices early and for the last time, has chosen to spend his afternoon reading Mary Shelley's *The Last Man* before the symphony. He underlines a passage that feels like a message from beyond: "I have lived. I have spent days and nights of festivity; I have joined in ambitious hopes, and exulted in victory: now—shut the door on the world, and build high the wall that is to separate me from the troubled scene enacted within its precincts."

Build high the wall. Viktor is at peace—or at least, he's ready. For the first time in years, he doesn't fear the sound of footsteps coming up the stairwell, and when it's time to get dressed, Viktor goes to his closet and pulls out the finest suit he's ever owned, the one he bought with Helen in Paris.

Viktor lays out the dark gray trousers and charcoal jacket on his bed and goes to the kitchen to heat a pot of water. His mother taught him this trick a long time ago, how to iron without an iron. He wipes down the wrinkled clothing with a hot, damp hand towel and uses his copy of *The Last Man* to flatten out the creases before heading to the symphony.

A black sedan with a Nazi license plate disperses the crowd in front of the ghetto's House of Culture. Although the sun is dipping below the horizon, the temperature in the ghetto is still rising. Elsa sits as close to the window as possible because Brandt's limp frame looms far too close in the back seat. Brandt is wearing an elegant all-black Hugo Boss suit designed by the Nazi fashion designer Karl Diebitsch. As per Brandt's request, Elsa is wearing her red dress, which means her bare back is sticking to the luxury sedan's hot leather upholstery.

So far, everything is going to plan. Elsa sent Tadeusz's old wardrobe to the Ghetto Workshops Bureau a few days ago, informed Singer of the plan, and paid him handsomely. Early tomorrow morning, Singer will help Viktor into the secret compartment before sending the wardrobe to Wymagamówka for delivery, where Elsa, Rachel, and the children will be waiting.

All that's left to do is find a way to inform Viktor.

"Careful, the air is infectious," Brandt says as the car comes to a halt. "After the driver helps me, you will wheel me straight into the building. No lingering. Now help me with the mask."

The driver hands Elsa two gas masks and once she's finished pulling the taut rubber head cap over her hair, she fixes Brandt's mask, steps out of the car, and waits for the driver to place Major Brandt into his wheelchair.

Concert-goers whisper to each other and recoil as Elsa wheels Brandt through the crowd with the hulking driver in tow. Brandt yells imperceptibly from within the rubbery gas mask as they reach an impasse at the foot of the stairs of the House of Culture.

Elsa leans in with her own bug-like face. "What did you say, Herr Brandt?"

"Get me up these stairs, now! I told them to build a ramp!"

The gawking crowd looks on as the driver lifts a furious Brandt into his arms. Elsa drags the empty wheelchair behind them and searches for Viktor in the crowd, but the hot, thick air of the gas mask's infernal tubing fogs her vision.

Viktor arrives to a surreal scene outside of the *Kulturhaus*: a hulking chauffeur has just finished carrying a Nazi officer up the symphony stairs with a slender woman in a red dress in tow. All three are wearing gas masks that make them look like bugs. *Could it be?* Viktor stands on his tiptoes and cranes his neck, but the three quickly disappear inside. *Impossible.*

He moves towards the entrance with the curious crowd, shuffling forward with other hollow-cheeked men who float inside their suits and adult women who appear adolescent in their oversized dresses. Everyone is asking the same question: why would an SS official enter the ghetto *now*? Let alone attend a *Jewish* symphony? A young man tells Viktor, "It's a good sign. They're willing to live with us again." A woman wearing a golden necklace says, "Don't be an idiot. It can only mean something wicked." But Viktor doesn't care to think about these questions—what a wonder it is to simply *hear* lively conversations in German, Polish, Yiddish, Hungarian, Czech, French, and Dutch, outside of a symphony, no less.

Viktor cranes his neck to try and spot Martin but the Ghetto Police is corralling the crowd with their whistles, pushing and shoving as they wade through the throng of symphony goers, ordering people to stay away from the Nazi vehicle parked in front of the theater.

As hundreds of people—*could there be thousands?*—press towards the House of Culture, Viktor finds a good vantage point atop the symphony steps. For an instant, he swears he can smell a familiar scent of orange blossom perfume; he spins around in search of the source.

She isn't there, but Viktor is nonetheless overcome with a sudden bashfulness as he takes in the beauty of all these women wearing their best summer dresses. He's transported to a time of youth and possibility and almost feels giddy amongst so many in their weekend best: elegant gowns, fedoras, and three-piece suits, clothing that flatters the ghostly figures of the people they used to be; and even if their bodies are wilted and sickly, tonight, they hold themselves with dignity.

Viktor waits like an attendant at the House of Culture's great wooden doors. He doesn't recognize most, but he is proud to be amongst them and is particularly taken by a woman with a short bob haircut who checks her makeup in a window's reflection. She applies her magenta lipstick with care and uses the corner of a white handkerchief to wipe away a smudge at the crease of her lips. A man in a tan suit with a boyish smile sneaks up to her; she squeals when she sees her lover in the window's reflection, jumps into his arms, and spreads her perfectly applied lipstick all over his face.

Yes, romance is still possible, even here in the Łódź Ghetto. Viktor is overcome with gratitude to be here now. How glorious it is to witness a couple kissing, and what bravery to dress up and come to the House of Culture despite everything, to discuss arias and Beethoven and Goethe and Schubert just a grenade's throw away from the ghetto's Central Prison.

Once in the foyer, *this exquisite, crowded foyer,* Viktor smells the orange blossom perfume again. He closes his eyes to better savor the scent, for in this fantasy, he sees Elsa clearly. *Her gaze may as well be fire. One glance would be enough.*

Viktor enters the auditorium and walks down the aisle towards the front, where Henryk has secured three seats right next to the orchestra pit. Viktor lays his jacket on the seat next to him, saving it for Martin.

Elsa wheels Major Brandt towards the impossibility of yet another flight of stairs while the driver goes outside to move the car. Brandt rages from his wheelchair at the bottom of the iron staircase leading to his private balcony. He demands assistance but refuses to allow any ghetto policeman to touch him.

"I will not be touched by *Untermenschen!*" He protests in fury.

"It will only take a second, Herr Brandt. These men can help."

Brandt huffs and puffs as two skinny ghetto policemen struggle to carry him up the narrow passage. They slip and fumble as they try to guide his lifeless feet up each step. Finally, a third, hulking ghetto policeman tells the others to make room as he slings Brandt over his shoulder and delivers him to his private lair.

Brandt curses his unwanted savior, but Elsa strokes his forearm and slowly calms him—she's learned to play her role well. "It's over, Herr Brandt. The champagne is coming."

Sure enough, a servant arrives with a cold bottle of champagne and two glasses. Elsa removes her gas mask first and takes her time helping Brandt, slowly prying the dry rubber off his sweaty, grimacing face, hooking his nose and pulling his hair in the process.

Brandt is red-faced by the time he gathers himself. He holds the champagne glass up to the light to admire the golden bubbles. "I had this bottle sent from Berlin. It's Salon, the *Fuhrer's* favorite."

Elsa ignores him, leaning forward on the balustrade and turning her attention to the audience. Viktor must be here. He has to be. Brandt says all council members were invited.

"Incredible, isn't it?" Brandt also leans forward. "They still have hope even after Rumkowski's speech. And look at how ghastly they're all dressed!"

Elsa takes a large sip of her champagne and lets her silence speak as she continues to scan the faces in the audience for any sign of Viktor.

"Miss Dietrich, a snack, perhaps?" Brandt offers a plate of carrots and pastries.

"No, thank you."

"Don't be rude. You can't drink champagne on an empty stomach. Now eat."

Elsa picks up a carrot and presses her bosom into the balcony railing to get as far away from Brandt as possible.

Elsa's face grows hot and her heart skips. She's just recognized someone from the Astoria Café, the former rabbi and Professor Henryk Dawidowicz.

"Excuse me, Herr Brandt. I'm all flushed from the champagne. I'll just go to the powder room before the symphony begins."

"Yes. The powder room. That's a fine idea," he says through his labored chewing.

Elsa leaves the private box and heads directly for the

lobby bar.

"Has anyone seen Viktor Bauman? Professor Viktor Bauman? Is he here?"

"He's sitting up front," someone says.

"No, he isn't," another retorts. "I'm sure he isn't coming tonight. Didn't you hear what happened to Martin Arendt?"

Elsa has no time to waste. She hurries into the auditorium, where the trumpeters are playing their scales and the pianist is playing single octave notes to help the others.

Elsa is halfway down the aisle when the gas-masked driver cuts her off. "I'm sorry, Madame," his voice reverberates through the rubber as he yanks at her arm. "It isn't safe for you down here without a mask. You must return to your seat."

He points up to the balcony, where Major Brandt is beckoning.

Elsa doubles back to the bar and scribbles a message in her notebook. She rips out the page and wraps it around a wad of cash to hand to the bartender.

"Can you make sure you deliver this message to Viktor Bauman? I heard he's sitting up front. He has kind eyes and will likely be with a large, bald man named Martin Arendt."

The bartender looks at the money and then at Elsa. "What's in it for me, beautiful? One thousand more złoty and maybe a kiss?"

Elsa smiles a cruel smile and fishes in her black purse for her Nazi Party card. "What is your name, bartender?"

The bartender looks horrified. "The money won't be

necessary, Madame. I apologize. Please, I didn't mean ... I have a family—"

"*What is your name?*" Elsa demands.

"Put—Putersznyt," the bartender stutters. "Please, I didn't mean—"

"If you want your family to survive tomorrow's deportation—*Putersznyt*, is it?" Elsa writes his name in her ledger. "Make sure Viktor Bauman receives this information *tonight*."

"Where's Martin?" Henryk points at the empty chair next to Viktor.

"He's probably at the bar. That man is never in a rush," Viktor says absentmindedly while making a paper airplane with the symphony's program, a habit he picked up as a child.

"Have some respect, Viktor," Henryk snatches the paper airplane and unfolds it to flatten against his thigh.

"Give that back," Viktor rolls the paper into a baton and taps it nervously on Martin's chair. "I'll find him at intermission. He's probably just late ..."

The human roar in the symphony hall begins to dwindle as the string players finish tuning their instruments. A bejeweled elderly woman sitting directly behind Martin's empty seat leans her head forward to occupy the space where Martin should be.

"Excuse me, professor? Professor Bauman?"

Viktor turns around. The woman is wearing multiple bracelets on both wrists and a gold necklace that jangles. Her perfume is overwhelmingly pungent with the sickly sweet smell of roses.

"It's a pleasure to see you again, Professor Bauman. My name is Madame Jakubowski. We've met before. As I'm sure you are aware, I used to be on the board of trustees at the university."

"Ah, yes," Viktor pretends to remember. "Nice to see you again, Madame Jakubowski." He turns back around, but she doesn't take the hint.

"Of course, as you know, with tonight's program of the *Erlkönig*," she speaks loudly into his ear. "There is the leit-motif of liberation and salvation throughout Goethe's work. But what do you think of Schopenhauer's philosophy in light of the current situation, Professor Bauman?"

"Schopenhauer? The situation? I'm sorry, Madame Jakubowski, but if you don't mind, I'd rather listen to the tuning of the instruments."

"Oh yes, the music, of course, me too!" Her face hovers next to him. "But of course, Beethoven is far inferior to Bach, in my opinion, when it comes to the use of repetition. Do you think it makes sense to pair Beethoven with Schubert's *Erlkönig*?"

"I apologize, Madame," Viktor turns abruptly and looks her in the eye. "I don't mean to be rude, but it's hard to appreciate the music over the sound of your voice. If you'd like to ask me the question during intermission, I'd be more than happy to speak to you."

Madame Jakubowski purses her lips and scoffs, her jewelry rattling as she harrumphs back into her seat.

Viktor closes his eyes to refocus on the final tuning of the strings but Madame Jakubowski is now jabbering away to her sleepy companion: "It is quite impossible, in fact, to understand Beethoven's Fifth without understanding Hegel's concept of the spirit. That's the trouble with music these days. There's no sense of *history*. If only people could—"

Viktor stands up from his seat and turns around. "Madame! You'll never understand anything if you keep trying to explain it. Hegel has *nothing to do with this*. Now, please, if you want to learn something, I'd suggest you shut up and listen."

The house lights dim just as Madame Jakubowski's face contorts in offense. Henryk chuckles and whispers to Viktor, "Martin would be impressed."

The audience goes silent and the conductor takes the stage.

The lights dim as soon as Elsa spots Viktor. In her excitement, Elsa spills her glass of champagne all over Brandt's lap, causing him to shriek and call for the servant, who arrives with a flashlight and a towel.

Viktor's frame is much smaller than it used to be, but she knows it's him—she can just make out his smile, illuminated by the warm glow of the orchestra pit.

Viktor glances over his right shoulder towards the commotion coming from the private balcony. A light beam slices through the dark, but he can only see a woman's silhouette.

Viktor turns his attention back to the pregnant stage, where the conductor clears his throat, holds his baton high in the air, and commands a perfect silence before a cascade of violins and cellos announces Beethoven's Fifth Symphony in C-minor, the world-famous four-note motif transporting Viktor elsewhere with the first two measures.

Brandt hisses at the usher to bring more champagne and is visibly confused by Elsa's excitement. Brandt is all but screaming into Elsa's ear as the music begins, but she leans further forward on the railing, willing Viktor to see her. *I'm here, Viktor. I'm here.*

"—soon be liquidated," Brandt's voice finally gains control over the music. "It's incredible, really. You must take your hat off to whoever decided on the *Erlkönig*. How delightfully wicked, a swan song about a monster that harvests children."

Elsa stands up from her seat. "I have to clean myself up, major. My feet are covered in champagne."

Brandt grabs onto her wrist. "It is going to be a busy autumn, Elsa. This is why I have brought you here with me. Do you understand? To witness it and see what lies ahead."

"Yes, Herr Brandt." She tries to wriggle herself away.

"Do you see, down there?" He maintains his grip. "The bacillus of civilization? We are doing the thankless work of the gods. It can never be discussed. It is like the *Reichsführer* said—'we are carrying out a most difficult task, and nobody in history can know'—but it is a testament to Aryans like me and you that we have suffered no defect. Now get yourself cleaned up so we can enjoy the symphony together, my sweet Elsa."

At the same exact moment, almost three hundred kilometers away, Carl stumbles outside the mess hall in Bilgoraj to have a smoke. The battalion has been drinking for many hours in preparation for tomorrow's special mission. The sky is a bluish purple, the air muggy and dense with flying insects. Carl puts a hand over his heart to feel the stack of Elsa's letters in his chest pocket, to all that remains left unsaid.

"The booze is a good sign," Carl slurs his words and struggles to light his cigarette. "Like I said, if they wanted us to do something difficult, they'd want us to be sober in the morning. Nothing to worry about, though. It's surely more of the same. We poison wells and look for ghosts. It's all it ever is. Ghosts is all it ever is. Remember that, Thomas."

Carl retires early to the barracks after emptying his bowels for the third time this evening. Soft moonshine bathes the bunkhouse in silver but does nothing to quell the taste of bile gurgling up his throat. Carl's body knows things his mind cannot yet grasp, which is perhaps why he goes to the window to peer outside and brush a cluster of sun-bleached cicada husks off the windowsill, adding to the pile of exoskeletons on the floor.

"I miss Elsa."

"You need water and rest," Thomas says. "Maybe stay behind tomorrow and finally send those letters to her? Tell her how you really feel. What do you think?"

"She'll think I'm a coward. I can't. Not yet."

Carl curls up in the fetal position and turns his back to Thomas.

"Thomas, are you afraid?"

"Afraid of what?"

"Afraid of tomorrow."

"Let's just focus on tonight. Think about the letters."

Carl pulls the letters from his coat pocket and throws them at Thomas. The loose leaves of paper flutter to the floor.

"Send them, Carl. If not for her, then for yourself."

Carl closes his eyes in search of Elsa, but he can only see orange and red splotches behind his eyelids. "It's no use. I can't remember how it used to be with her. How do I get back there?"

Silence.

Carl turns around. "Thomas?" He peers over the edge of the top bunk, but there's only a shimmering pile of crushed insects glowing in the moonlight.

Like a pendulum swing to the other side, some three hundred kilometers back in the other direction, Viktor remains frozen in his seat. Here at the House of Culture, Viktor transcends place and time, forgetting who he is, who he was, and who he once thought he should be. Here at the symphony, he forgets about the Gestapo cellar, deportation lists, and the authorities' demand for the children. Instead, he submits to this infinite moment of brevity, wonder, and playful innocence, relieved to know this kind of bliss need not be named, analyzed, qualified, or debated. Everything is in its right place at the symphony, tucked within the small miracles of suppressed coughs and soft tears. Here in the auditorium, Viktor anticipates the standing ovation, which will rise and fall as the music ends, where hundreds of fellow spectators will file down the aisle having been changed fundamentally.

Who amongst them will return to the memory of this night in the days to come? Who will survive? Will it happen tomorrow? Will there be an intermission? A reprieve? Amidst the music, Viktor realizes time is only ever flowing through him, for he is being held by something more than the sum of trumpets and strings and a cello's harmony, and what a relief to know that in this moment he can simply *just be.*

The thunderous applause sends a great trembling down his spine. In a daze, he stands up to join the crowd as it floats down the aisles for intermission. Standing in euphoria in the reception area, Viktor remembers he needs to find Martin.

"Has anyone seen Martin Arendt? The former chess master? Anybody?"

Viktor sifts through the crowd to the front of the bustling bar. "Have you seen a grumpy old bald man who probably stinks of vodka? His name is Martin Arendt. Can you tell him Viktor is looking for him if he comes around?"

The bartender looks surprised and relieved. "Viktor Bauman?"

"Yes."

"Thank God!" The bartender hands Viktor a crumpled paper. "A nasty Nazi woman told me to give this to you. Tell her Putersznyt did his job. I don't want any trouble."

"What are you talking about?"

"Just take it, sir. Putersznyt. Say my name. I don't want any trouble."

Confused, Viktor takes the note and unfolds it:

Ghetto workshop tomorrow 5 A.M. Foreman will let you in wardrobe. Ghetto to be liquidated. So we may meet in more amicable circumstances. E

In Bilgoraj, the night is calm save the nightmares and the crickets. The barracks are putrid with belches and worn boots and a five-hundred-man battalion's stench. Carl is neither awake nor asleep. In hopes of slumber, he contorts his body into variations of the fetal position to no avail.

Respite only comes when a commander's shouts at the men to get out of bed. "You have ten minutes! Bring your rifles! You'll get your orders at the destination. Hurry! And no questions."

Flashlights illuminate the dark barracks of groggy reservists searching for weapons, ammo, and shoes. Outside, Carl falls into rank alongside the others, waiting to pile into idling trucks. He peers down the line in search of Thomas. No luck.

Carl, Cornelius, and a sixteen-year-old recruit are ordered to load ammunition crates into the truck beds.

"Hey! You," the commander says to the boy, "Stay here and guard the barracks."

"But I'm ready, sir," the boy says.

"You're not ready!" The commander screeches. "I'm doing you a favor. Now *stay here.* That's an order."

Carl wants to step forward, hoping the commander might give him the same reprieve, but Cornelius pulls him backward and laughs at those who stay behind.

"Fucking greenhorns!" He yells over the revving of truck engines. "We'll take care of it! Just make sure there's plenty to drink when we get back!"

The youngest recruits load barrels of lye into the trucks, their diesel-fueled engines filling the air with black exhaust. The sun is just beginning to crest over the horizon as Carl's truck lurches forth. He steadies his rifle between his legs as the battalion begins its descent.

freedom

"Set me like a seal upon thy heart, love is as strong as death."

—Viktor Frankl, *Man's Search for Meaning*, 1946

Martin never made it to the symphony, but Viktor doesn't have time to make much sense of it. He hurries back home and packs a small bag—a notebook, a pen, an extra scarf, a sweater—and slips into the predawn light. As he creeps along the shadows of the ghetto, he listens for the syncopated march of ghetto patrols, hugging his body tight to the labyrinthine walls and passageways. His mind is void of expectation or worry. His feet are determined to complete his task. By first light, Viktor reaches the main road leading to the ghetto workshop.

The morning is warm and the streets are thick with the slop from the latrine wagons, but the air isn't sweltering, not yet. Viktor trots along the road but doesn't run lest he rouse suspicion. When he reaches the main ghetto workshop, he goes to the back entrance and knocks on a flimsy windowpane of an even flimsier wooden door.

A tall, thin man with gaunt eyes and calloused hands greets him. "Bauman, right? We don't have much time. Come in."

The foreman looks right and then left and locks the door behind him. Viktor enters a large room with high rusted ceilings. The soot covering the two massive skylights only allows small beams of dappled light to enter. Viktor follows the foreman across the empty warehouse floor, the motors and cutting machines idle, waiting for their masters to begin the day's work. The smell of pine tar and wood char fills each inhale as they pass dozens of expertly-crafted wooden tables and bookshelves, ornate cabinets, and other custom wares to be sent to wealthy oppressors unbothered by filling their homes with crafts made by "the enemy." Many of the items are plastered with shipping labels to various destinations: Munich, Warsaw, Hamburg, Wannsee, Dresden, Rotterdam, Strasbourg, Vichy and Paris.

The foreman stops and points to a familiar wardrobe. Its sign reads DESTINATION: WYMAGAMÓWKA.

"Stretch your legs and say a prayer and get in, Bauman. The day's shift starts in five minutes."

Viktor is stunned. He drags his hand along the carved wood and recalls Tadeusz's last words.

"I'll tell your mother you said hello."

"What?"

"Nothing," Viktor beams.

"Come and see," the foreman steps into the wardrobe and shows Viktor the small finger hole in the secret panel. "It's quite the piece. Tadeusz did great work. We repaired the secret latch to open from within. The drive will take about four hours."

"Wait. Did Martin Arendt come in yesterday?"

Singer shakes his head. "He was a dead man walking, Bauman. But I heard he put up a hell of a fight. Quick, get in."

Singer unceremoniously presses Viktor into the secret compartment and slides the door shut without another word.

Viktor wriggles himself into a semblance of comfort with his body flush against the back panel and his nose squished up against the door.

The stifled darkness and the heat of the wardrobe make him dizzy. Viktor calms himself with deep, rhythmic breathing and decides to believe that Martin might still be alive, somehow, might still be snoring next to Viktor's bookshelf.

On the other side of the wardrobe, the foreman knocks three times. "Everything's ready. You're out for shipment. Don't leave the wardrobe until you know you're safe."

"How will I know?"

The wood muffles Viktor's voice. "Hello? How will I know!"

The factory bell rings. "This one's ready!"

Two hundred and seventy kilometers away, Carl's truck navigates a gravel road along the Vistula River. Because of the unpaved roads, the thirty-five-kilometer drive from Bilgoraj takes almost two hours during which Carl watches the silhouettes of white houses and thatched-roof villages rise and fall against the backdrop of a flaming sky.

He reaches beneath his shirt to feel at his pounding heart and realizes his stack of letters for Elsa is no longer with him.

"You threw them at me last night," Thomas says. "Remember?"

"I forgot to pick them up before we left."

"Don't worry. You can write them again. Whatever you forget isn't worth remembering, anyway."

"Shut up and drink this," Cornelius hands Carl a canteen of lightning water.

"Everybody out," the commander speaks softly. "Keep your voices down. They aren't awake yet."

Carl jumps down from the truck and feels the liquid amphetamines kicking in. His heart is racing. The battalion gathers around their commander in a half-moon formation.

"Something's wrong with him," Thomas says. "The major looks pale."

"I told you to *shut up*," Cornelius says. "What the hell's gotten into you?"

Carl watches his nervous commander turn over a piece of paper in trembling hands. The commander gnaws at the inside of his cheek, bites his fingernails, peers down at his shuffling feet, does everything he can to avoid reading the paper.

Thomas is right. Something's wrong.

"Welcome to Wymagamówka, men. Today we've been ordered to …" the commander trails off. "Know that I didn't ask for this responsibility …"

The commander clears his throat and, with tears in his eyes, gives the orders. "It is a regrettable situation, I admit, but it comes from the highest of authorities. There are eighteen hundred Jews in this village and further confirmed reports of partisans in the area. The future of the fatherland—the future of your children, of your children's children—depends on us. If it makes it any easier, remember, the enemy's bombs are falling on women and children in Berlin."

The silverfish in Carl's stomach has reached the base of his esophagus.

Thomas is the voice of Carl's fear. "He's not saying what I think he is, is he?"

Just a few kilometers away, Elsa's black sedan arrives at the farm outside Wymagamówka. She's late.

She peers into the barn. "Rachel? Wladyslaw?" She climbs up to the hayloft to find empty tins and milk bottles.

"Miss Dietrich!" Wladyslaw hisses at her. "Come quickly. Something's happening."

Elsa hurries back down the ladder. "It's good to see you, Wladyslaw. The delivery left on time. Everything's going to plan."

"We can't talk here," Wladyslaw's voice trembles. "Put the car in the barn and get inside the house. A friend just called from town—a heavily armed German unit is gathering in the square."

Elsa moves the car into the barn and, with Wladyslaw's help, closes the large red barn doors. He leads her down into the farmhouse's cellar, where Little Tadeusz runs out from beneath a table to jump into her arms. Elsa can't help but hug the boy back, even as his mother pries him off of her and reprimands him, slapping the boy in the face.

"Never leave your hiding place unless I give you permission!" Rachel hisses. "What did I tell you about the skeleton men!"

Little Tadeusz begins to cry. Rachel holds back her tears.

"Come here, my child," Wladyslaw picks up the wailing boy and takes him to a far corner of the cellar.

Rachel's eyes are white with terror. "We're not safe here. The neighbors came looking for us last night in the barn. We have to leave."

"It's not safe out there either," Elsa explains. "I got stuck behind a column of troop transports coming here. We'll wait for Viktor and leave tonight."

"Uncle Viktor?" Little Ania asks. "Is he coming?"

"Yes, he is! He'll be here soon."

"He'll be here soon," Rachel repeats. "And then we'll go to the forest. He'll be here soon ..."

It becomes a mantra, almost a prayer. *He'll be here soon.*

Wladyslaw loads his hunting rifle. The children are silent. Rachel is restless but Elsa is patient.

He'll be here soon. He'll be here soon.

Viktor twists his knees and cricks his neck to reposition himself in the speeding darkness. He focuses on his body vibrating to the rhythm of the machine and recalls the music from the symphony to distract him from the pain. In the shifting phantasmagoria behind his eyelids—explosions of purple, yellow, and orange—Viktor ignores his aching bones, screaming ligaments, and taut joints; he focuses instead on the thought of Elsa—*she was there*—and on the white noise of the truck barreling towards its destination.

The situation is tense and eerily quiet in the Wymagamówka village square. Carl squeezes his eyes shut to try and block out the sound of a baby crying through an open window.

The commander speaks with a tight throat. "We will round up the men of working age and deport them to labor camps. The remaining people—the remaining Jews— including all of the women, children, and elderly are to be shot. But remember, men: we must shoot them, not torment them. There is a difference. We shall do it with honor. They will dig their graves in the forest on the edge of town."

Carl begins to fidget with many other anxious reservists. He knew this town *used* to be a partisan stronghold, but killing women and children at point-blank range? What have they done? Do they deserve it?

Carl searches for Thomas in the crowd.

"Where'd Thomas go?" He asks Cornelius.

"Who the hell are you talking about?"

Confused, Carl looks around wildly, but all he sees is fear in the other men's faces.

"It isn't fair," one of them says. "This isn't our job."

"I'm just a store clerk," says another.

"I thought we were only rounding up partisans!"

"I'm not a killer! I didn't sign up to shoot babies."

A few dozen SS men form a circle around the apprehensive reservists, jeering like hyenas as the commander presents the battalion with an extraordinary choice.

"Those who do not feel up to this task are permitted to excuse themselves. All I ask is that you do it now. Raise your hand or step forward. Nothing will come of it—I promise—but please choose quickly. We have a long day ahead of us."

"We can't do this," Thomas' voice is loud in Carl's head. "We aren't murderers, Carl. We can't do this."

"Of course you can!" Cornelius has a firm grip on the back of Carl's neck.

Carl's stomach heaves. He bends down and puts his hands on his knees, trying to expel the creature crawling up his throat. From this vantage point, doubled-over, Carl can only see dusty boots stepping in one direction or another. His head is teeming with voices, beliefs, and convictions. His skin is itching from the amphetamines.

Carl stands up straight and looks for Thomas. "Where'd he go?"

Carl watches one man step forward, and then another, and then one more as SS men shove them about. Carl wants to step out, too, but Cornelius' grip is firm on his neck. Carl wriggles away from Cornelius and plunges his finger down his throat, but there's no silverfish in the end, only wretch.

Cornelius loosens his grip. "I'm proud of you, soldier." Horrified, Carl sees himself standing frozen while the twelve men who stepped aside are escorted away. And now, he and the remaining men are led to a demonstration area where a doctor wearing a white lab coat mounts a white canvas onto a wooden easel and draws a diagram outlining human shoulders and a head.

Like a deranged painter, the doctor explains how to properly execute a human being with a bullet to the nape of the neck.

"You should place the fixed bayonet here as an aiming

guide, but whatever you do, don't shoot the head unless you want to make a real mess of it."

Cornelius puts his arm around Carl's shoulders. "You're finally going to pop your cherry. I can't believe you've made it this far without shooting any *Untermenschen*."

A smiling SS man approaches Carl and Cornelius. "Good morning, Landau. You're sprightly, as always! Is this your shooting partner for the day?"

"Yes. His name's Becker."

"Good. Choose a squad and inspect the farmland, would you? There are reports of families hiding in nearby farms."

"Yes, officer. Shall we do them there? Or bring them back here?"

"I don't see any need to complicate things. You've seen the demonstration—not that you need it, Landau!" The officer jokes. "Just get it done quickly. We'll need you back here to help with the rest."

Carl's vision flickers. He has trouble remaining upright.

"Don't worry," Cornelius says. "Shooting feels like vomiting. You'll feel better afterward. I promise."

"Can we bring Thomas with us?"

"Who the fuck is Thomas?"

"The young one. From Danzig."

"You're drunk. Do you need more Pervitin? Keep it together."

"No. I need Thomas. He can come with us. He's my friend."

"Your friend? You don't have any friends out here, Carl. I'm the only person you've got."

During Viktor's impossible sleep inside the secret wardrobe, he dreams he's floating inside an egg. The egg itself is floating, too, weightless within some deeper darkness. Though it's dark inside the egg, it isn't the absence of light, not exactly. The darkness is visible—it can be interacted with. Within this void both quiet and deafening, it isn't the absence of noise, either, not exactly, but the roar of complete silence. Viktor hears himself swallow for the first time—the sound of a miracle—and listens to the sound of his lungs compressing and the pumping valves of his heart. He hears the sound of his muscles and organs contracting, feels the strength of his trachea, the fibers of his tongue and the lubricated ligaments of his oropharynx working together. He is a symphony unto himself.

A sudden stillness before the external world interrupts this internal crescendo. It is an engulfing vibration, like the thunder of a waterfall or the roar of a great wave. Viktor tightens his eyes and tries to return to the egg, but as he awakens in the actual darkness of the wardrobe, what he hears is the sound of a cooling engine, passenger doors being opened and closed, muffled voices accompanying their owners' footsteps, and now the unlatching of a metallic bolt and the sliding open of a heavy door. Viktor is lifted upwards. A momentary sense of weightlessness. And amidst all of this—*is it possible?*—the scent of orange blossom perfume.

Printed in Great Britain
by Amazon